Sweet Favors

Love Happens • Book Six

SUSAN WARNER

Sweet Favors

One

"Spiders and dust bunnies I'm okay with, but if I reach up here and find Mickey, there's going to be a problem."

Katherine Gerald climbed up the rolling ladder in an attempt to retrieve the ledger book from the top shelf in the courthouse library. While it was someone's genius idea to put the oldest books at the top, they obviously hadn't considered how they were going to retrieve them since they were all stacked upon each other horizontally. Wouldn't it figure the day Sandra Waters, the owner of the community center, wanted to review the records for the building, the clerk had called out sick? Katherine had two options: reschedule this meeting that had been a nightmare to coordinate or get herself up the ladder that looked like it could only support a five-year-old at best.

"Are you the one?" Katherine asked as she wiped away a layer of dust from the tome. "No, of course you're not the one; the huge one at the very bottom of the pile is the one."

Katherine reached up with both hands to move the book, and the ladder rocked beneath her weight.

She tried to brace her feet on the rung. Instead of feeling more secure, she was greeted by the creaks and groans of old wood held together by dovetail edges and faith.

"I'm already up here, so I'm going to make it count," Katherine said as she reached for the book. That was when she saw them. Two beady eyes staring back at her and a small gray body that almost blended in with the dust on the shelves. She gasped when she saw it, and that shook her so much she had to grab the shaking ladder until it stopped moving.

"I'll spot you," called a voice from below. "I'll hold the ladder steady."

Katherine dropped her head against the rung. "Joe come lately to the rescue," she said to herself. "A man always shows up when I'm almost done with the task. They must all have synchronized watches to come right at the end."

Katherine looked over her shoulder and saw a man in a blue shirt holding the ladder. "I'm about done," she told him as she pulled the book off of the shelf. "You're not needed, thank you."

"The ladder is old and shaky; it's no problem for me to hold it," the man said from below.

"Really, I'm good," she replied, agitated as she balanced the book on the top rung of the ladder.

Katherine decided enough was enough. She didn't want to see Mickey, and there was something annoying about the man who wouldn't move and had come entirely too late. Moving the book from one rung to another, she began to climb down the ladder. Every step brought with it its own set of creaks and groans. By the time she had gone three rungs, she had realized the rungs were getting narrower as she went down and they wouldn't be able to hold the book.

There was nothing left to do but to cradle to the book to her chest. She tried not to think about how all the dust would be pressed against her black suit jacket. If her allergies weren't bothering her before, they would be when she finished fishing this book down. When she thought she had it firmly in her grasp, she inched one foot down the ladder. The ladder groaned; the book was heavier than she thought, and it began to slide down the front of her chest.

"I'm just not going to get a break today," she muttered.

"Don't worry, I'm spotting you!" the guy said.

Katherine thought about how she'd really like to toss the book down at him and say catch! The book was too old, and the pages would never survive. Spotting her now was like bringing a towel to a flood.

"I'm just about down," she said. "Just back up so I don't accidentally kick you."

"You won't kick me. Here, let me help you."

Before she could say anything, she felt a pair of strong hands go about her waist. He grabbed her to steady her, but the shock of him touching her made her jump. The book wobbled to the side. She followed the book. She leaned too much to the side, and the heel of her black short kit heels got caught on the rung, throwing her off balance.

Katherine's thought was only for the book that she hugged to her body, and she hoped whoever the late Galahad was had some cushion to him.

When she was sure the fall was over, she opened her eyes. She did a self-inventory first. She wiggled her feet, took a deep breath, and then sneezed from the dust she'd inhaled from the book firmly in her arms. The book was safe. Katherine was trying to think of an appropriate way to move off of the late Galahad when she was abruptly rolled onto the floor.

Of course, when he rolled her onto the floor, she went face first into the dusty book. She didn't know who he was, but when she got up, she was going to give him a piece of her mind. Pushing herself up to her knees, she found herself face to face with Vihaan Higgins.

Well, he did have enough cushion on him to take her weight, and none of it was fat. So this late Galahad she had a history with. Vihaan Higgins had to be the poster child for the beauty of children from mixed marriages. He was the best of all worlds. He had dark, thick black hair that was never out of place. His skin was bronzed all year long, giving him a look that made every day seem like a day to go on vacation. On top of that, he had the most beautiful eyes. She had heard members of his own family tease him about it, but it couldn't be denied. Women would kill for those chocolate brown eyes framed with the longest lashes she had ever seen naturally. Just when it couldn't get any better, there was the fact that Vihaan was considered the nicest guy you could work with.

Vihaan Higgins was an amazing architect. He mixed his Indian background with a solid foundation of beauty and efficiency. He was starting to make a name for himself, and everyone knew it was only a matter of time before he left Sweet Blooms. His mother Geeta owned the Banter House restaurant, and when he was published in Architect Today as an up and coming architect, she bought copies and gave them out for free to the customers of her restaurant.

She'd met Vihaan because both of them had worked on the design of Adam Cade's woodworking building. She was Adam's Cade's project manager for Sweet Blooms. Work would be the catalyst to bring them together again. Sandra Waters, the owner of the community center, had convinced Adam to help her renovate the community center. That meant she needed a project manager and an architect.

Katherine had to admit Vihaan had an air of professionalism and talent that gave her pause, and she wondered if she would be able to keep up.

He pushed back a lock of hair that had fallen into his face and gave her a smile that every woman over the age of 25 would swoon for.

"Hello, Katherine the smart," he said. "I was just in time."

Then it came back to her when he called her that nickname why she thought he was the most arrogant and pompous person on the planet. "In time would have been before I got on the ladder."

His smile widened when he said, "It was fate that you climbed the ladder so I could break your fall."

Getting to her feet, she shook her head at his logic. Then she realized what had happened. "Your hands, are they okay? Your mother will kill me if I've injured you in any way."

"The only injury I have is to my heart. It's pained that you feel I was late."

"No, Vihaan, this isn't a feeling. It's a fact. You weren't here when I had to climb the ladder. On top of that, when you did get here, and I told you to move, you didn't listen. Instead, you grabbed me, threw me off balance, and then I had to fall on you."

He was still smiling at her. This time he had his arms open as if he was waiting for a hug. "To be clear, I did not grab. What I did was steady you on the very old ladder. The reason why you fell is because of the very impractical footwear that you chose to wear on the ladder."

She did a double take of her footwear. "My footwear?"

Katherine heard someone else clear their throat.

"Do you have the book?"

"Yes, I do have the book, and thank you for helping me up," Katherine said, doing her best to keep her tone even. Her mother always told her to keep an even tone. People responded better when a young lady kept her composure. Katherine still wasn't sure about that rule, but she was doing her best.

Determined not to be swayed from the current target in front of her, she once again faced Vihaan. "My footwear, by the way, is amazing. The heel is a sensible three quarters. The color is a versatile black, and they are so comfortable I've been able to run for public transportation in them. I agree there is a problem, but it is not my footwear as you pointed out.

Now that she had gotten that statement off her chest, it was on to the issue at hand. When Katherine turned around to face Ms. Waters, she was confronted by a new group of people. In fact, one of the people she spied standing behind Sandra Waters was Percy Smalls, the presumed sick intern who was the county clerk for the court library.

Percy was 18 years old if he was a day older. In his hands, he had a breakfast sandwich And a large hub of take-out coffee.

"I know it looks bad," Percy said around the food in his mouth. "And I want to say that I did wake up this morning not feeling very well."

Katherine held up one of her hands to stop him before he launched into a long explanation. "It was fine. I know how to find the books in the library. And I also know how to find the ladder if I have to."

Then, as if no more insult could be added to this injury, Vihaan spoke up.

"Percy, don't worry, I was already here to save her from hitting the ground."

"I'm told that sometimes people who are geniuses in one area have difficulty in another. You did not have to save me from hitting the ground. I would not have needed any saving if you had left me alone."

Katherine thought for sure by now he had gotten the hint. She was wrong. Instead of understanding what she was saying, Vihaan took it a whole different way.

"So, you think I am a genius?"

"Oh, I do think you are one of a kind."

"That's good, because that is exactly what I think about you too."

Katherine was speechless. Instead of replying, she turned her back to him and then muttered under her breath, "Breathe. If I just breathe, it'll get better; just one breath at a time."

Then, as she was about to put this whole incident behind her, she felt him wiping down her legs. Katherine whipped around to face him. Vihaan was kneeling on the floor, and when she turned around, the corner of the book hit him in the head.

"Ow!" Vihaan said.

"What?" Katherine said. Vihaan fell back on his butt

on the floor. Katherine looked at him and said through clenched teeth, "What were you doing?"

"I was trying to get the dust off the bottom of your pants. I knew you could not reach it with the book still in your hands."

The first problem was that Katherine was very sensitive about her height. She was a full five feet tall. Vihaan sported a height of five feet eight inches; not that that was very tall, but it was still taller than she was. Vihaan had a talent in pointing out all of the things she was the most sensitive about. The second problem was this was not the first time she had met him.

At the end of the last project the two of them worked on, he decided to tell her a revelation that he had found out about her. He said he had heard lots of people comment on how cute and small she was, but he was very happy to find that she was also a very intelligent woman. When she didn't look like she was thrilled with the compliment, he immediately tried to make it better. He followed it up with another comment about how he had heard that she was not smart, just that she was very attractive. At that point, she'd put her hand up and told him to stop while he was ahead and then walked away.

It seemed to clear to Katherine that he'd been given a body that everybody would like to make up for his poor communication skills.

Katherine understood who and what she was. Many a person had been taken in by her small stature and her youthful face. After she laid out her plans for a project, they soon understood that compact package hid a general. Adam Cade was her boss, and he liked to call her his secret weapon. When projects were slowed, and only excuses were being given to him, he sent her to fix the problem. She could bargain with the best of them. Katherine had a poker face that made people doubt what they knew. She was knowledgeable. She was efficient. And she was ruthlessly diligent until she got the project done.

"Katherine?"

"Yes!"

Vihaan looked at her, holding the book over his head. "Do you have the book securely in your arms, and can I get up now?"

Katherine hefted the book up into her arms and then took a step back. Vihaan stood up and brushed the dust off of his pants. "This is no problem now; we can go and work." He extended his hand out to show her the way and let her go first. "Ladies first."

Work? Katherine's confused look must have shown up on her face.

"Haven't they told you?"

"Told me what?" Katherine demanded.

"I am working on the community center project with you."

Katherine turned to look at Sandra Waters, who just shrugged. "They told me I needed an architect, and we knew him."

Katherine needed a fast-acting vice, she thought. She didn't like spending money, and she didn't like eating a lot of sweets. The one thing that Katherine loved to do was read. She'd read anything—magazines, books, and journals; it didn't really matter.

Then she looked up into the waiting gaze of Vihaan, and she felt a little flutter in her stomach. Vihaan was fast-acting. He quickly got on her last nerve. She could still acknowledge that he was an attractive man; he just wasn't the man for her.

Vihaan had called his family together to his house. Everyone knew his projects were starting to get a lot of attention. He knew his mother, Geeta, had been talking with his aunt Anika about what company he should go with and what that would mean to the family. He had made a decision. For support, he had called his cousin Suhana to the meeting as well.

Now, as he straightened up his living room and prepared for them to come, he wanted to make sure he had all the pamphlets, statistics, and plans in case anyone asked. He was preparing not just to let them know what he was going to do for a job but what he intended to do as a career.

He would prefer to showcase one of his architectural projects rather than present to his family. He had always been the child in between, and today he was going to confirm that he didn't favor one side or the other. It was hard growing up in a family that had a mixed culture. Both sides watched you like a hawk, wondering which side you would take after. When you did something that didn't fit comfortably with either side, you always ran the risk of being alone and misunderstood.

Vihaan made sure to set up a place for his father to sit where his back would be supported. Vihaan and his father had an odd relationship by all accounts. His father, Jerry, never understood why he wanted to draw all day, but he let him do it. When he said he wanted to become an architect, his father didn't agree, but he paid for him to go and to travel outside the United States to see other architects.

He'd made his wishes clear that he wanted Vihaan to get a "real" job in building or construction, or even go back to school to become an engineer. When Vihaan said that path wasn't for him, his father had shaken his head and then told him, "Make your way then."

Now Vihaan was going to share with his family the "way" he wanted to go. It would affect everyone, and he hoped they would be supportive.

The bell rang, and he took a deep breath before letting them in. His mother, Geeta, grabbed him and kissed him first before practically giving him to his aunt, Anika. Anika kissed him on the cheeks and then took his face in her hands before tugging his hair and saying it was too long. His father came in behind Anika and gave him a nod before seeking out a place to sit. Last was his cousin, Suhana. She was wide-eyed and all smiles. She enveloped him in her arms and kissed him on both cheeks before whispering in his ear, "Is she here?"

Vihaan smiled. "No, and behave yourself. Hopefully you will still be talking to me afterward."

"Cousin, don't be silly. I'll talk to you no matter what. Who else will be my partner in crime?"

Vihaan closed the door and then turned to make sure his father had found his place.

"Please, everyone get comfortable," he said. He looked out at his family and reminded himself they were his family. They didn't have to agree all the time, but they would support him.

"I wanted to let everyone know that I have received three offers of employment from the top three architecture firms in New York."

All of the women in the room jumped up and clapped. They hugged each other and kissed each other. Then, as if they remembered he was in the room, they ran to him and hugged him as well. The only one who didn't move was his father.

Vihaan saw his mother run to his father and say, "Jerry, you have to be happy about the news?"

"If that was the news that he brought us to hear, I might be happy, but it seems as though there's more that he needs to be telling."

His mother stopped jumping around and turned to look at him. Then the other two women turned as they realized he wasn't done with his news.

His aunt was the first to speak. "What else could you want to tell us?"

He cleared his throat and looked at everyone in the room. "Dad is right; there is something else I need to tell everyone. I've made a decision not to accept any of the job offers. Instead, I want to stay here in Sweet Blooms and open up my own architectural firm."

There was a pregnant pause in the room, and then, out of nowhere, his dad began to laugh. Suhana looked at his father, and she too joined in the laughter here. Again, his mother and his aunt both looked as if they weren't sure if this was real.

As soon as it became clear that he was serious, Anika was the first one to recover. "You can't just walk away from those big companies. Don't you know that's good money you're passing up? You will always have time to go ahead and open up your own business. If you do it now, no one will come to you. You don't have a following yet. Just because you were in the paper once or twice doesn't mean that you are good enough to be on your own yet."

He had expected this response from Anika, so it was no surprise. The person's response that he was really waiting for, the one that really mattered, was his mother's. His mother's response wasn't as quick as Anika's. Instead of accusing him of anything or telling him what he could or could not do, she paused and gave him a long look.

"Why Sweet Blooms?" she asked.

"Adam Cade has offered me an opportunity to work with him in building up the county of Sweet Blooms. I didn't want to be his employee, so I decided I would stay home and open my own business. When I have finished working on all of the projects, then, if my business isn't working out, I'll go and find a job."

His mother smiled. "Well, I will say this, it's nothing if not interesting. Whatever you decide, you know I will be with you."

"You can't tell him that!" Anika spat. "He should take the job offer with one of the big three companies. Why would you let him die in this town when he could be so much better?"

The room went silent, and Vihaan had heard enough.

"Aunt Anika, I understand you are disappointed. I know you wanted someone to go on and do greater things, but I need to do what is best for me."

"No, Vihaan, that is not the way. I know you feel as though you are a man in between two worlds, but you have an obligation to your family to do the best you can. When you went to school, your parents took out money to support you. When you went overseas, they sent you the extra money you didn't have. Now, when you have the opportunity to not only clear that debt but to take care of them, you choose to stay in Sweet Blooms?! That is not acceptable! Geeta, tell him!"

"My son has paid me."

His mother and aunt both turned to his father. He wasn't going to say anything. It wasn't his place to say it, but he had given his father half of every bonus, check, and income he had been given to make sure he paid them back for their sacrifice.

When he had sent the first payment, his father had returned it. After a long discussion, his father had relented. Still, it wasn't Vihaan's place to tell anyone, and so he waited for his father.

Suhana was still all smiles as she looked at the ensuing drama. When no one else spoke, she ran to him and hugged him.

"I'm so happy for you, Vihaan. I'm happy that you are staying local and happy that you are still doing something you love. We've all seen Cade building in the surrounding area; you have to tell me what you are going to be working on."

The next two hours passed with everyone asking questions about what was being built and when all the new people who had commissioned the projects were coming. His father seemed content with the news. His mother was happy as long as he said he was happy. Suhana was Suhana. As for his aunt Anika, she didn't disagree with anything that was said, but she wasn't participating in the discussion either.

When they were leaving, his dad patted him on the back and said good luck. His aunt Anika hugged him and told him she hoped he knew what he was doing. His dad was leading Anika to the car when his mother stopped and looked him in the eye.

"I would be interested in the real reason you are staying in Sweet Blooms when you feel ready to tell me." With that, she kissed him on the cheek and left. Suhana was right behind her and the last to leave.

"I just want to meet this woman who is worth three, not one or two, but three New York job offers."

Two

Katherine double-checked that she was at the right address. The night before, she had received a meeting invite. The message had been sent out by Adam Cade. He wanted her and Vihaan to meet at the new training center. It was his thought that he wanted the Community Center to match the theme and the feel of the training center.

At first, when she saw the message, she was a little offended. She didn't need to have the architect on site to review a site. She could take a basic structure and the functionality and duplicate it anywhere. Ultimately, she would be responsible for the purse strings. It only muddied the waters to have too many cooks in the kitchen.

Still, Adam was her boss, and she knew he understood small towns much better than she did, being she was from the city. Katherine had been Sweet Blooms for about two months. She was still trying to get used to the silence of a small town. At nine o'clock, everything went to sleep. After living in the city for more than ten years, she was used to the hustle and bustle of a town that never slept.

At five o'clock in the morning, the birds started chirping. She was still amazed that they were real birds and not pigeons. She stepped out of her air-conditioned compact car and into the morning heat of Florida. She looked around and found she was the only one standing in front of the community center. She looked at her watch, and sure enough, it was nine. She waited, and the next time she looked at her watch, it was 9:10. If he had any hope of showing her a better side of himself, it had gone by ten minutes ago.

Just when she was sure she was going to do the walkthrough herself, she saw a massive orange and blue truck coming down the block. It wasn't racing, nor did it appear to be in any rush. She looked up and down the block and didn't see one parking space the monster truck could fit. As the truck pulled up next to her compact, she prepared herself to hear the excuses he would give for being late, and she waited to hear him ask for a little bit of time while he parked the monster truck.

Instead, the truck pulled up right next to her compact car and parked. She saw him put on his hazard lights, and then he stepped out of the truck as if he were on time. Vihaan Higgins had an easy smile and a slow key when he greeted her.

"Are you ready to go ahead and take this tour?" he asked.

What she really wanted to say was, "Yes, I am ready to take the tour. Oh, but I was here on time and ready at nine o'clock." She could already tell it was going to be a problem with schedules. She tried to keep an open mind; besides, she was the New Girl in town. Vihaan was loved by everyone in town. Katherine remembered this was worth it; it wasn't personal, and she didn't have to like the person in order to work with them.

Once she moved past his lack of punctuality, she had to take a moment to look at how he was dressed. He had on a very long shirt that ended right about mid-thigh. The shirt clung to his shoulders and was a breathtaking orange. Beneath the long shirt, he wore a pair of dark jeans. The outfit was completed with a pair of brown thong sandals. "I'll try to make this quick; I can see that you have plans."

He took a moment and looked over his clothing after she had finished speaking. Then he gave her a smile that would have made even the fiercest woman melt. "No, Katherine, I have no plans. I'm all yours today."

He turned around and took out his key fob. The next thing she heard was the total sign of the car being locked. Katherine took the opportunity to look at her clothes. Like every day, she had on a pair of black pants, a white top, and her matching jacket was sitting in the car. Katherine had never learned how to master the magic of color coordination. She fixed that problem by coming into work with the same outfit every day—dark black pants, a white top, and a magical black jacket.

Katherine tried not to focus on their differences. Right now, they needed to get a project done. The training center was newly built, so it would be fairly easy to copy the workflow and design. The sooner she got this job done, the sooner the both of them could go their separate ways.

He got to training center first and held the door open for her. Once again, he meant to surprise her. She hadn't expected him to have any old world manners.

"Thank you."

"I see you thought I didn't know the basics of how to treat a woman due to our prior meetings?" he said. "Don't worry, I took a refresher, and my mother has tasked me with impressing you with only my best behavior."

"It's your choice."

As soon as she walked into the training center, she was accosted by color.

"Exciting," he said as they walked through the center.

She wasn't sure she would have used the word exciting, but she could definitely say she wasn't tired. They continued to walk down the hall and into one of the classrooms. All the while, she was taking notes and trying to get her head around what she was seeing.

"So I thought we were going to collaborate during this meeting?"

"I don't usually collaborate. I'm just here to make sure the project is on time and under budget."

"I don't think so."

"Okay so much for being politically correct and polite. Why don't you say what you mean?" she said sarcastically.

"Good or bad, we should talk about everything."

"Oh, you mean like yesterday when it was very clear you don't know how to take instructions?"

Vihaan shrugged. "Poor footwear choice."

Katherine shook her head. "Think whatever you like, but I was practically born in kit heels."

"Then it must have been very shocking for you not to be able to balance yourself on the ladder."

Violence is never an answer, she thought as she gripped her pocketbook while she looked at his head. He wanted to talk. He didn't take instructions well.

And now he wanted to change the process that she had used on every other successful project she'd done. This meeting was only temporary. Maybe if she let him talk, he would get it out of his system and then she would be able to go back to doing her project planning. Katherine thought about it. She was more than willing to pay up front now for peace later on.

That hope was short lived. As soon as they went into the next room, he started asking her questions. He asked questions like how many people could he have on the team? Was there a team to be assigned to each room in the community center? Did she like the shapes of the rooms, and what did she think about removing load bearing walls for the sake of space?

She was both impressed and horrified by all of his questions. All of his questions spoke of his experience in building a new structure, and all of them were expensive. The more questions he asked, and the more he talked, the more she saw her budget growing.

While she had answers for most of the questions, some of them she said she would have to get back to him about. "It's good to know I'm working with someone who is knowledgeable about the process."

Vihaan smiled, and she smiled back at him. "That way, you won't be surprised when I say no to certain purchases."

It took him a moment to process, but when he did, he just laughed. Katherine didn't have a good feel for Vihaan, and she felt like she was going to need it.

"You are an odd duck, Vihaan."

"There are worse things to be."

She gave him another look. "Not that I listen to gossip, but I might have heard it mentioned that you are turning down some city jobs to stay in Sweet Blooms."

Vihaan smiled. "Yes, that's true. I think everything I need is here in Sweet Blooms."

"Really? Everything? Maybe you aren't dreaming big enough," she said.

"I think the biggest things a person can have is family and love. I have both of those things here."

"Ah," she said, shaking her head.

"You don't agree?"

"I'm the wrong person to ask about either one of those things. I don't do family, as mine is spread all over the United States. We don't really get along, so for the sake of us being able to talk to each other, we don't stay around each other. As for love, if I want that, I'll buy a pet."

"I'm an architect because I love to do it."

"I'm a project manager because I'm good at it."

Vihaan nodded. "You might be surprised, Katherine. I think you love it as well."

"It would be a surprise to me. So let me get this straight. You passed up making a lot of money working in the city to do…?"

"To make my own hours, choose which projects I want, and try to have some work-life balance."

Katherine nodded. "There are those things."

"Besides, I know a secret."

"What?"

"If I'm talented today, I'll be talented tomorrow. So if this all goes south, I'm sure someone will hire me to do some desk work," he said with a grin.

"It's not like you just left college. You've got an impressive resume of projects."

Vihaan bowed. "Thank you. Let's take a moment and gather our thoughts."

Katherine wasn't really sure what that meant, but she was willing to work with him. They took a seat inside one of the training rooms and began to talk.

"Your home is in the city?"

Katherine shook her head. "I don't have a home, really. I travel so much. I think I've spent, at most, a solid two weeks in my place that I'm renting."

"I've done most of my work outside of Sweet Blooms."

Katherine looked at him oddly. "So doing the design for the center will be a change for you?"

"Budget-wise, but I know everyone here, so it's not a problem."

Katherine took a moment to really look at him. He was a handsome man, no matter when she looked at him. He had the confidence and experience, and there was just something about him that just drew her to him. At the end of the day, she figured he had to be a really confident man to come out with those brown thong sandals on.

If she was honest, she would say it wasn't the sandals that really made her see him. It was his blatant ability to put on any color and feel confident. There was something about him being able to wear any color at all that made him seem more intriguing. He said that he was staying in Sweet Blooms for love. She thought about what he said, and the more she thought about it, she knew. If there was a person out there for her, he would like the same two colors she liked—black and white.

"Have you always been a project manager?" he asked.

"No," she laughed. "I actually started out working in the court system, and I used to have a job as a process server."

"You?!"

"Yes. The reason I was so good at my job was that no one ever suspected I was there to serve them court papers. But I did it for about a year, and the money was okay, but I wasn't going to make a career of it. I thought about paralegal, and then I got a job with a moving company. I stayed there and did logistics for a while, and then someone said I should try project management. I did, and it paid, and I stayed in it."

"I can see you went a long way but wound up in the right place. My aunt would say you need to suffer before you find the thing you are good at. It's a good sign; you'll stay longer."

Katherine laughed. "How does that rule work for you?"

"It doesn't. I've always wanted to be an architect. My parents have always supported my dreams. But she still has hope that the most important thing in my life that I really want will make me jump through hoops and suffer."

"I hear nothing but good things about you. Anyone would give you a hand. If she says you need to suffer, you will definitely have to leave Sweet Blooms."

"Well, I've said no to the big city, so Sweet Blooms is all I have now."

Katherine stared at him.

"Go ahead and ask," he encouraged.

"You've been working in the city and in other places that are a lot just more than Sweet Blooms. How can you know you'd be happy here?"

"Because what I want is here."

"How do you know Sweet Blooms is ready for your style?"

"My style?"

Katherine looked at him and motioned from his head to his feet.

He looked confused. "You mean my American slash Indian mix style?"

"I haven't been here long, but I can say in some ways Sweet Blooms is stuck in time. That's part of its charm, but that can be a problem as well."

"What are you saying?"

"I'm saying that the town is rooted in deep traditions, and some of your choices might have to be modified to fit those ideals. Are you ready to do that?"

Vihaan looked at her for a minute before answering. "Are you saying my Indian style might not be welcome in the community center?"

"I'm not saying no, but what I am saying is people don't come to Sweet Blooms or live in Sweet Blooms because they are looking for cutting edge diversity."

His face went blank, and Katherine regretted the choice of words, but it was done. "That sounds a lot like you want me to design whatever the masses want and not my vision."

"It could wind up being something to that effect."

Vihaan nodded and then stood up. "I thank you for your time. I think we have done enough collaborating for the day." With that, he walked out the door, and she heard his truck beep, start up, and rev away.

Katherine sighed. She didn't make the rules, but it had to be said, didn't it?

Three

The offices of Cade Designs were being run out of what were now two temporary buildings on the Cade property. One of them was for the incoming crew, and the other one was occupied by Katherine. Now that the woodworking building was done, Cade had given her office space in the temporary shelter. When she came in, she realized that there was another person already in the better cubicle, but she was okay with that. The divider walls were high so she wouldn't even see them. Besides, she liked the way her office was because her door faced the main hallway into the building.

Waiting to get in early and set up her items, she was at her space by seven. She enjoyed the quiet at work. It helped her organize her thoughts. She was a creature of habit, so setting up all of her items was very important. She had to have her desk calendar on her desk and another calendar on the wall. The computer had to be on her right, and she had to have a wall behind her.

She had been in the space for an hour, and she was sure that all was well, but still, she wasn't content. She started shifting things a centimeter here or a centimeter there. When she started to indulge in this type of OCD, she knew it was because her head wasn't in the game. Unfortunately, she also knew the root cause of her scattered thoughts: Vihaan.

As she lay in bed last night, she did a review of her behavior, and she found that she had let her personal bias and fears run amok. She had no problem with people from different cultures or backgrounds, but she did have a problem when it came to colors. All through her life, there had always been random comments that it was such a shame that such a pretty girl had no sense of style or color. It was one of the reasons she shied away from parties and decorating anything.

Now here she was, a respected woman in her field, and she had let her childish fear blind her. Whenever she got scared, she looked for weaknesses in the opposition. Working with Vihaan, she wasn't going to be able to avoid it. She would admit that she had considered not doing the project, but what answer could she give to Adam?

"I'm sorry, Adam, I can't do this project because I'm intimidated by colors?"

Even before she finished that thought, it was taken off the table. So, early this morning, her brain had decided to step up and give a resolution. She would stick with the numbers and project timelines and give Vihaan the range he needed to, as he said, "create his vision."

The easy part was arguing with herself and coming up with the answer. The hard part was going to be how to fix this with Vihaan. Acting like she hadn't said anything wasn't an option. She had to figure out how to make amends and for them to move on.

She thought she could try to meet with him after the

meeting they had scheduled today. He attention was drawn to the click of the front door, and who should be coming in but the man she had been thinking about—Vihaan.

Did this man wake up ready to do a cover shoot? Not that she was interested in him in that way, but once again, he was the example in the dictionary as a modern drool-worthy man. He looked like he had just gotten out of bed. His hair had that messy look everyone was trying to get with gel. He had on a red shirt that had a vee in it that played peekaboo with the bronze skin beneath it. It was confirmed that Vihaan worked out. He might be a talented thinker, but he didn't neglect his body. He wasn't her type, but that didn't mean she couldn't appreciate an attractive man, and right now, she could confirm Vihaan Higgins was one of those men.

Vihaan let the door close behind him, and when he lifted his head up, he was looking directly at her. He stood still, and all of the emotion drained from his face. She remembered how Vihaan would always have a smile for everyone, but she had taken that away with her small-mindedness and selfishness.

Katherine had prided herself on sticking with the facts. Giving everyone a fair shake, but all of that went to the wayside when she panicked. She knew what had to be done, and she was glad that he was here for her to do it.

She came around her desk and met him midway down the hall. "I was wrong."

She waited for him to agree or disagree. Instead, he just stood there and waited. Katherine didn't like the way he just stood there.

"I'm not good with the guilt thing. Are you going to accept my apology?"

"Was that an apology?"

Katherine shook her head. "I'm saying I was wrong and that I shouldn't have said that to you. It was my baggage coming out."

He nodded at her and then walked by and went to the other office. She followed him as if she were a groupie at a concert. When he took his seat, she could see all the signs she couldn't before. On the wall was a picture of an Architecture Today magazine. On the desk was a little miniature house.

"This is your office," she said matter of factly.

"Yes."

"I should have known."

"Yes, you should have."

Katherine heard his clipped tones and stood at his doorway with her arms over her chest.

He looked up from his desk. "Yes?"

"Is this the way it's going to be?"

Vihaan cocked his head to the side and then let out a breath. "I was shocked, Katherine."

She looked away. "If it's any consolation, and it may not be, I was shocked too."

He got up and went to stand in front of her. "If it was a shock to you too, then maybe there's some work to be done."

"You think you can help me out?"

"Since we're doing a project together, I'll do this for you, and I won't charge you extra."

Katherine laughed. "You are too kind."

"I'm glad you are finally noticing that."

"Enough! I have work to do, and Vihaan?"

"Yes?"

"Thanks."

The rest of the morning went without a hitch. Vihaan stuck his head in around eleven to say he had to look at something and would meet her at the community center at three. Everything was back on track. Katherine was sure that from here on out, everything would be fine.

Katherine was sure she was going to kill Vihaan before the meeting ended.

The meeting had started out like every other meeting. Per Sandra Waters' request, they had it at the community center. Katherine could tell she was dealing with a businesswoman when she arrived at the scheduled room. The room was barely habitable. Sandra Waters wanted to make a point about how much work the center needed, and she had chosen a room that was the poster child for why they should gut the room.

When Katherine walked into the room, there was the faint odor of dampness. It wasn't overwhelming, but it was just enough for you to look at your seat before you sat. If you did, you'd find yourself looking at a rug that had definitely seen better days. Katherine had to look twice before she realized that the rug didn't have a speckled design on it; those were old stains. The chairs were new, as was the table in the room, and it only served as a sharp contrast to the walls. Katherine could see they were uneven.

When everyone arrived, Sandra started giving her pitch on why she thought an exorbitant amount of money was needed to fix the center.

"Have either of you ever been to the Cade shop?" Sandra asked.

"Yes, we work there in a temporary building," Katherine replied. Katherine knew where this was going, and she wanted to head her off at the pass. Sandra paused, but then she went forward with her demonstration. Sandra stood up in the middle of the room and motioned to the current surroundings of the room they were in.

"Well, the point that I was trying to make is, the community center has to be able to compete with the Cade building when it comes to services and offering a pleasant environment. Look around this room. To get us where we need to be, we have to be sure we are investing enough." When she looked at Katherine and didn't see any type of agreement, she looked to Vihaan who was nodding his head.

That was the first thing that happened. Katherine put that on her to-do list when she spoke with Vihaan later. One should never give the client any indication that they know what is best. In fact, their ideas should be classified as suggestions that will be taken into consideration, but it should always be clear that the project manager will have the final say. Sandra Waters smiled at Vihaan and then took her seat. Then Vihaan spoke.

"I completely agree that these conditions are not optimal for the business."

Katherine put her hand up and caught their attention.

"Let us remember, the community center isn't competing with Cade's workshop. They are in two separate lines of business. The shop provides a set of services, and some of those services overlap with the classes here at the center. But the center provides a range of services that the shop does not, so while I understand that concern, we are here to make sure we shore up your image and not create one that would compete and/or overshadow Cade's workshop."

If it was possible that looks could kill, Katherine knew she would have been a goner. Sandra Waters turned to her, and her whole expression became pinched.

"Now, can we move on?" Katherine asked. "Vihaan?"

After that moment, Katherine thought the ground rules had been set; she was wrong.

"Ms. Waters, I can tell you are very concerned about how much care will be devoted to your place."

Care? Katherine was writing down another note on her pad that she kept out for meetings. The word care sounded too wide for interpretation. In fact, when she heard those words, she saw the budget of the project ballooning.

"I want to assure that we are going to keep to the vision and feel of the community center," he said. Sandra preened, and Katherine internally groaned.

That would be the second thing he did that made Katherine have to bite her tongue. Was he giving guarantees? How could he do such a thing? She just had to get through this meeting. If she took deep breaths, she could make it to the end of this meeting without reaching over to grab him by his gorgeous throat.

Vihaan had come in with a whole bunch of drawings, but that was okay; she knew today was proof of concept only. After Sandra's theatrics, it appeared that Vihaan was ready to show the proofs.

The first set of pictures were just what Katherine was hoping to see. Sandra Waters' shoulders slumped with the pictures, and she could see that she gave a polite nod and every now and again. The pictures outlined how all of the rooms would be painted in neutral colors. The furniture would be standard so that if chairs or tables needed to be moved from one place to another, they could all be interchangeable. When he was done showing the proofs, he asked Sandra what she thought.

Sandra looked at both parties with a less than enthused look.

"I think that these are okay options, but this doesn't really capture the spirit of the community center."

Katherine winced when she said the spirit of the community center. Those words sounded like she didn't think enough money was being spent in the center. Katherine thought the design was fine, and she was giving Vihaan redemption points for his earlier two faux pas. Then it went downhill again.

"I can see this is not what you were thinking. Perhaps you'd like to see my other option?" Vihaan said.

Sandra nodded. "Yes, please."

Katherine wanted to reach across the table and tell Vihaan no, that option one was good. She knew there was going to a shift because when she flipped to the next page in the book Vihaan had given out, she was assaulted by the colors in the book. She looked at it and several more pages past it, and she was wondering if she was even looking at the same building.

She knew Sandra liked it from the oohs and aahhs that followed. Vihaan went on to explain how, in his vision, the community center was the heart of the community, and it beat with a life of its own.

Katherine just heard the sound of more money going

into the budget. Vihaan wanted every room to have its own distinctive color and theme. The furniture would be eclectic and multi-colored so they'd fit in every room. The building would have to be modified, of course, in order to accommodate the open spaces he thought needed to be there for creativity to flow. Oh, and of course there would need to be some major rewiring done to accommodate for the transitional lighting and the track lighting that would be throughout the whole building.

By the time they were done, Katherine was sure the thing had gone, at a minimum, twenty-five percent over the budget. Being able to source the colors he wanted as well as find the contractors he needed in order to move the beams into the right place might push the project into twice the time allotted. By the end of the meeting, Katherine had at least four pages of notes that were really questions on how they were going to accomplish most of the items that Vihaan had said. They rambled on and on without regard to time or money. Once or twice, she had tried to reach out and kick Vihaan under the table to bring him back to his senses, but nothing worked. If he felt the kicks at all, he didn't stop talking.

Then she supposed he got the wrong idea, so he tried to incorporate her into the conversation.

"What do you think about this color for the children's programs?" he asked her. Katherine just nodded and said it wasn't her vision that was being promoted, so it was more of a Sandra question. Like best friends, they talked about color and feelings. Katherine just took notes and nodded. She was once again the odd girl out. Now it was worse because even

Vihan, as masculine and gorgeous as he was, seemed to be more in tune with his creativity than her.

Finally, she gave up and decided to bide her time. She and Vihaan would have a conversation on reviewing options before they presented them to the client.

Four

Katherine couldn't get out of the room quick enough. After all of the hands were shaken and the promise that they'd be back to look over next steps, Katherine made a beeline to her car. She heard Vihaan call her name. When he thought they should talk, she instead told him she'd meet him back at the office.

She told herself not to take what happened personally. How long had she been a part of groups and hadn't been able to participate because she wasn't girly enough? Katherine remembered all of the taunts about how a pretty girl couldn't pick pretty. She remembered picking a dress for prom thinking it looked good and everyone else thinking it was a joke. Other times her color choice was too loud, not matching, just off, or in some cases, just ugly.

She'd compensated by relying on her other skills, but she hadn't expected to be pulled into a color question. She was so frustrated, and she just wanted to drive. Katherine knew she had to go back to the office eventually. She started her car up and took the long way to get to the Cade ranch.

Twenty minutes later, she was in front of her office.

The monster truck was already there, and when she got out of the car, there was no heat coming from the hood. Vihaan must have come directly back.

The first thing she noticed was the smell of food. She went down the hall and into the main room of the trailer, and there was a miniature eat-in kitchen. She looked around in wonder.

"Hello, Katherine. You left before I could invite you to lunch, so I brought it here since I knew you'd come back," Vihaan said.

"How do you know that I didn't already eat lunch?" she asked. She knew she was being difficult, but she hadn't found an answer to a problem that obviously wasn't going to go away. Now she felt like a heel on top of everything else. Here he was being extremely kind to her and looking good while he was doing it, and she was just a pain.

"I don't know that, but I'd be a great person to eat with now."

Vihaan smiled at her and then pulled out a chair from the table.

"Please do me the honor. Even now, in the state you think you are in, it would be a pleasure to eat with you."

His whole demeanor caught her off guard. When she went to take the seat, he pushed her seat in, and his hand lightly brushed past her shoulders. The touch and his comment made her super aware of him as a man. Then he made sure her food was in front of her, got her a drink, and then took his seat.

Why would it even matter if he touched her or not? Probably because she couldn't remember the last time a man touched her besides to shake her hand before a business deal. Had she really been working that hard?

He sat across from her, and he looked at her. She was confused, and then he nodded towards her food with a smile on his face.

Katherine looked at the plate, and then it came to her.

"You're waiting for me to eat?"

Vihaan's smile transformed into a full grin.

"Yes, Katherine, it will always be you first."

"I know this is going to sound rude, but is English your first language?"

"Yes, it is, and I'm told I'm really good at it too," he said with a wide smile on his face.

"Okay, so I'm the one who looks ignorant now?"

"No, I could never see you that way, but it tells me other things."

She picked up the hamburger in front of her and took a bite out of it. She didn't realize how hungry she was. Then it came to her why she liked this burger so much. It was just the way she liked it—medium rare with mushrooms and avocado. She swallowed the bite and looked up at him.

"It must be telling you a whole lot because this burger is exactly the way I like it."

He held up his hands. "I'm not stalking you, Katherine. You are a creature of habit; whenever we ordered lunch working on the woodworking shop, you ordered the same thing every time."

She scrunched her eyebrows together, trying to recall. "I guess I never realized it."

"It's fine. You've already explained consistency is a part of your nature."

"Wow, if you're like this with everyone, there must be something really wrong with you."

"I never thought about it like that, but I can say the problem is I already have a picture in my head of the woman I'm looking for."

"Ahhh, you're picky. I guess you can afford to be."

Vihaan laughed. "That's one way to say it. I have a question for you."

"Go for it."

"You weren't happy today," he began.

"No, but it was a combination of a lot of things. I told you about my concerns when it comes to color. The other issue was when you presented the first option, I thought it was fine. Then I saw the second option, and it seemed like you and Sandra saw the light and the vision, so I went along with it."

Vihaan had a contemplative look on his face. "I have to say that every time we are together, you always say what you are thinking. I thought it would be the same here."

Katherine took a breath and let it out. "In New York, if I offend people or come off as being too brash, it's not a big problem because it's the city. Here, things are different. It's a small town, and because of that, I need to work on, if not fitting in, making sure I don't offend too many people. In order for me to be effective, I need to be able to interact with the people here on Cade's behalf."

He nodded. "Everything you say is true, but it's also true that if you give in to them all the time, they will keep pushing you to give more and more until there's no more you, and that would be a loss to us all."

He sounded so sincere, as if he believed that she would be a loss. It caused a fluttering in her stomach when he said things like that. It was a feeling of being looked at and being seen as more. She waited for him to continue.

"Katherine, you have to know that not everyone gets along, not even in a small town, but what does happen is we adjust, adapt, and then we can appreciate the beauty that each one of us brings. Be you and make them appreciate your inner beauty.

Katherine swallowed and looked away from his intense gaze. She nodded.

"Funny, that's something I would tell my first-year project managers."

He smiled. "Maybe there's something about Sweet Blooms that makes you feel like you're starting over."

"Okay, let's not lose our minds. I thought I had to handle the people in Sweet Blooms differently than I do in the city, and you're right, I don't. Thank you."

"It was my pleasure to tell you something helpful, as I felt as though I was the cause of the pain earlier."

She felt a smile break out across her face, and she hoped she wasn't blinking her eyes like some cow on television. "You are on the road to making amends. Besides, I have to own a part of that and find a way to adjust."

Katherine realized she was staring at him a little too long and picked up her burger and began to eat. When she thought she had her head down long enough, she looked up to find him staring at her.

"What?" she asked defensively.

"It seems like you aren't making friends in Sweet Blooms the way you should."

Katherine snorted. "Yes, Mr. Observant, I just told you that."

"I know the answer."

Katherine looked at the gleam in his eye. "No, I don't think so, Vihaan. When people try to take me to social events so I can meet and greet, it never goes well."

"Ah, that is where I am different. I know someone who would love to be your friend."

Katherine looked at him for a moment, and when she realized he wasn't kidding, she burst out laughing.

"Why are you laughing?"

"Vihaan, you can't tell someone to be my friend. We aren't in school where people will be my friend because they want to date you."

Vihaan looked confused. "I can guarantee she doesn't want to date me. But if you are offended by the idea, I'm sorry."

It was one bite of her sandwich and maybe five seconds of silence, and the guilt was building up.

"Okay, tell me who it is," she said and then took another bite. She needed it so she wouldn't accidentally scream about how bad an idea this was.

She saw his smile get wider, and he relaxed back into his chair.

"She is beautiful, kind, and very considerate," he started. "A true free spirit."

Katherine's stomach was tightening with each adjective he used.

"A woman with so many great qualities. Why aren't you two together?"

Vihaan grinned. "You've asked that already. I think you are asking for personal reasons?"

Katherine eyed him. "Yes, they're personal. I would hate to run off the girl you like, and then your vision is corrupted for my project."

"It is my cousin Suhana, and I will ask her to give you a call. You two will get along wonderfully."

Katherine looked at him, confused. "Vihaan, we can't make her like me. I think we need to wait and see what happens."

"Well, you two are a lot alike, and the other thing is if one person likes you in Sweet Blooms, it starts an avalanche of liking. There is no one more likable than Suhana. Family means a lot in Sweet Blooms and to me."

Katherine smiled. "I think we all know that after you turned down all of those job offers."

"Money comes and goes, but family will always stay with you."

She listened to the sincerity and belief in his voice. Vihaan was a contradiction. She just wasn't sure she could figure him out and keep herself safe.

When lunch was over, she helped him clean and then promised she would bring lunch the next time.

"The day has been very full. Why don't we start tomorrow? It will give me time to sketch out some of the things you brought up so we can go over price and scheduling."

Katherine nodded, and they both walked out to the front of the Cade ranch. When they got there, and Katherine nodded towards her car, Vihaan asked her to hold on. He ran to his truck and then came back with something wrapped in paper. It was a flower.

She looked at him strangely as he extended the flower to her.

"Okay, what is this for?"

"Earlier today, I knew you weren't happy, but you didn't show it during the meeting or stop the meeting.

I thought of this flower. It's called the astilbe. It is very hardy, and you can put it in the ground when you get home. It represents resilience and patience. And I thought of you when I saw it."

"Thank you, I think," she said with a smile.

"Think of it as a sweet favor."

"A sweet favor?"

"It's an expression my grandmother told me. A sweet favor is something given by another with only the best intentions."

Katherine nodded. "Thank you again." Then she turned and went to her car. Okay, it was time to keep it real. If she didn't like him before, she could say she liked his style at a minimum. A flower. Who would have thought a flower would so move her.

True to his word, two days later, Suhana found her.

When Katherine found out she would be doing long-term work at Sweet Blooms, she moved out of the hotel and into a rental. It was a nice starter house with two bedrooms. She would have called it a railroad house if the back door and front door had lined up. In this case, the back door was on an extension and faced east while the front door faced north. Katherine thought it was a nice, out of the way rental. There wasn't much traffic on the street at all. All of those things lined up with her preference for privacy.

When Suhana found her, that was all over. It started in the morning with a double beep on a horn. Katherine looked out of the living room window and saw a small, beautiful woman waving wildly from Vihaan's truck.

"Are you Katherine?"

Shocked that so much sound could come out of such a little woman, she nodded. Then the woman got out of the truck and came walking down the path to her door. Now that she was out of the car, Katherine could see she was even smaller than she originally thought. She had jet black hair that had been cut pixie short. She wore blue jeans and a bright red shirt with what looked like gold trim.

Katherine had the door open by the time she got there.

Suhana extended her hand and poked her head in the door all at the same time. "Hello, Katherine," she said right before she pulled her into an embrace for a hug. When she let her go, Suhana had a wide grin and bright-eyed expression.

"We are going to be such good friends."

"You've got to be Suhana."

Suhana beamed. "I am. I am here to take you to work and get to know you."

Katherine smiled. "Are you always this enthusiastic about doing whatever it is Vihaan asks?"

"He so rarely asks for anything. I admit I am always eager to see what is important enough for him to ask, period."

"So, you are here because…?"

"I am here because he asked me, and second of all, I'm just entirely too nosey to let this go."

"Too nosy?"

"My cousin asked me to be friends with a woman who he has not brought to the house yet. And every time I ask him if she is a friend of his, he just stutters. Oh, yes, I was definitely coming to meet you."

"Well, please come in and have a seat. I still have to get some items before we can leave and I can go to work."

Katherine stepped back so that so Suhana could walk completely into the house. She watched her walk around and look from side to side, and for once, Katherine looked at the house as a stranger might look at it.

The walls were still white from when she moved in, and there were still one or two boxes sitting in the corner that had not been unpacked. The furniture was black—every piece of it, from the sofa to the love seat to the ottoman. The only color in the whole room was the brown of the wood television stand and the two end tables on each side of the couch.

Suhana walked into the middle of the living room, and then she turned to face Katherine.

"Did you just move in?"

Katherine shook her head no. Her stomach started to clench as she watched Suhana walk through the first floor.

"Has Vihaan seen your place yet?"

Katherine shook her head no again.

Suhana laughed. "It just gets better and better. If we stay here any longer, I'll make you late for work. Let me go get the truck started, and then I'll wait for you outside."

Katherine looked confused. "Get the truck started? You make it sound like it has to warm up."

"It doesn't have to warm up. I just need to remember which one is the brake and which one is the gas. I thought I'd do that without you being in the car. Hurry, I'll be outside."

By the time she had gotten into the truck, the engine

was running, and Suhana was smiling. They managed to drive in silence up until the first light. Then Suhana spoke.

"Are you ready," she asked.

"Ready for what?"

"Ready for the questions that everyone wants to ask, but they are too polite to?"

Katherine laughed. "I guess that's not one of your issues?"

Suhana shook her head vigorously. "I want you to know I do have issues, but being transparent and asking blunt questions is not part of that."

Katherine sat back and waited. This she knew how to deal with, someone who knew how to speak plainly. "Go for it."

"So what's going on between you and Vihaan?"

Katherine thought she had been prepared for any question, but obviously not, as she choked hearing this one. "Work. Nothing but work."

"So, you're not even friends?"

"Of course we're friends."

"So you do something more than work?"

"We're friends at work."

"So how many other friends are there at work?"

"What kind of question is that?"

"The question was if you and Vihaan are friends at work. I think that's great. I just want to know how many other people or friends work with you too."

Katherine thought about it. "We are the only two at work. Everyone else is in the other building or doing construction."

"So you two friends will have to work closely together."

Katherine groaned. "You make it sound like something else is going on."

"I'm just asking questions. Remember, I'm the new friend."

"I can see how people get tripped up by that cuteness of yours."

"It's true. It happens all the time, but I'm glad you recognized it. You see, we are going to be amazing friends."

Suhana grinned. "I grow on you, I promise."

Katherine smiled. "So do barnacles, and no one wants those."

"Think of me like coral. Everyone wants the pretty coral around."

Five

"Thank you, thank you," Tahani said as Suhana pulled her towards the front door. "I know Suhana said you wouldn't mind, but do you?"

Vihaan laughed. "It would seem my cousin's reputation precedes her. I'm good; you two go practice for the wedding. I will wait for Aadheep to get in from work, and then I will leave. It's no bother."

"You're sure?" Tahani was at the door looking for confirmation from Vihaan.

"Aadheep said he would be home soon. Maybe I should wait?" Vihaan could see Tahani struggling with the idea of waiting for her husband or leaving him with the kids.

"Go, you're already late."

"The children are already in bed." She tried to explain every now and again, looking at the clock and the door.

Suhana grabbed Tahani by the arm and pulled her out of the door. "If Vihaan does not know how to take care of children now, we are all in trouble. He is the back-up babysitter for everybody. He may be a big architect in the city, but here he's family. And with no kids, it means he is the babysitter. So come, come, we have to go."

Tahani mouthed "thank you again" as she went out the door.

Suhana was right. He was used to this. Suhana called him hours ago and said Tahani's husband was working late. Tonight was the practice for some cousin's wedding. She also told him she had volunteered him to watch Tahani's children. It was his pleasure to say yes.

After they had gone, he walked into the living room. As soon as he walked into the living room, it was clear there were children in the house. A truck was in the middle of the living room and a foot away; it was all laying on the floor. These were the signs that he was hoping to have in his house one day.

He knew that they had three children—one boy and two girls. Every time he came over, the girls were dressed up in party dresses, and every day was a tea day. Children had always been a part of his family. A child was a joy that everyone wanted a hand in loving and raising. But as time has gone by, getting a good job was no longer an issue. He had gotten past the hurdle of working long nights to prove himself, and he wanted something more. The idea of a family was becoming more attractive to him.

At his last assignment, he had made the decision that he wanted to find a wife. With the right woman, he would be more than happy to have children. If Sweet Blooms had been a larger town, looking for a wife wouldn't have been such a big issue. However, he had been on several dates, and they had all been the same. All of the women thought he was attractive, sweet, and had a stable income. Before the end of the night was over, though, he was placed firmly in the friend zone, or even worse, he was looked on as a brother.

His mother had told him to be patient. She told him that even though it looked like nothing was happening, the reason that he had to wait so long for someone was because she would be very special. He was actually about to give up and take a job in the city. It didn't matter which one. He was just going to take the one with the most money. He figured if he went to the city, he should certainly be able to find a wife there. But, as usual, his mother was right. The same day that he received all of the job offers in writing with a thirty day consideration clause was also the same day he met Katherine.

He heard the jangling of keys. Then the front door opened and there was the man of the hour. He saw him and grinned.

"Aahdeep, you are home," Vihaan said.

"I am, and I have to tell you, you are a big letdown from seeing my wife's face."

"Well, you would have, but she had to go to a wedding rehearsal. Suhana made sure she wasn't late."

Aahdeep winced. "Your cousin is very persuasive."

Vihaan laughed. "That is the most diplomatic thing I've ever heard said about Suhana. At any rate, they ran out and left me here to guard your gems."

Aahdeep grinned wide. "They are that. I heard you were turning down money to stay in Sweet Blooms."

Vihaan nodded.

"I wish you the best with your new business."

Vihaan laughed. "You sound like you are sending me to my funeral instead of going to make money."

"Do you regret staying close to home?"

He grinned. "Noe a single moment. Tahani and the kids give me something I couldn't find anywhere else. They love me unconditionally, and the kids are a joy and horror in their own right."

Aahdeep stopped and slapped his forehead.

"What did you do that for?"

"I should have realized earlier. You are turning down money, and you have the glazed look in your eye of a man who has found a woman."

"A glazed look?"

"Oh yes, the one that says she can make it all better. All the things she does now are beautiful and inspired by her love of you."

Both men laughed.

Vihaan stayed a little longer. He listened to the tales of the children and Tahani. He looked at Aahdeep and knew this was what he wanted as well. The joy and fulfillment he had that money couldn't simulate. Then his cousin tapped him on the shoulder.

"Have you told your mother or Anika?"

Vihaan shook his head no.

"Ouch! Soon?"

"It all depends on the woman I've fallen for."

"Well, I don't envy you. You haven't told the mothers. This doesn't usually go well."

"The woman I'm going after is not like other women."

Aahdeep shook his head. "Poor sap, he has truly fallen in love. Already he starts with how she is like no other woman in the world. Well, let me tell you this. I may not know the woman, but I do know you bought a flower from Daisy's. If I know, everyone will know in a matter of days, and they will all want to know. Pray you tell the mothers before they figure it out by themselves."

She was waiting for him outside the house on the porch. She stood in front of her door, wringing her hands together with a fake smile on her face, waiting for him to make it to the steps.

"I want to prepare you before you go in the house. Suhana has been in the house, and judging from her reaction, I'm thinking what's inside is not what you might expect either."

Vihaan smiled and walked slowly up the steps. He took his hands and placed them over hers to stop her from wringing them. He looked her in the eye and smiled at her.

"I know you don't believe me now, but I already know what's inside your house."

"Really?"

"Really."

"How can you know what's inside if you've never been here? Did Suhana give you a detailed description?"

"She didn't have to. I know you don't know this, but your cubicle probably looks a lot like your house."

"No—" Katherine started to deny it. Then, when he saw her thinking about it, she nodded. "Okay, you're right. That takes a whole load off of my mind. Let's go in."

Katherine's house wasn't surprising. When he walked in, the house was dark. The colors were dark, and his cousin had already told him there was little to no color in the place at all. He didn't think that it was a dismal thing at all. When he looked at the house, what he saw was the same thing he saw when he saw Katherine; he saw that she just needed time to grow.

They hadn't had a lot of time together. Even though they worked in the same building, he was always out trying to get things for the community center. She was always working on numbers. So it had actually been two days since they'd seen each other. Today, though, she had left him a message saying she wanted to meet him at her house.

"Have a seat. I wanna ask you something, and I need to build myself up to it."

Vihaan was curious about what could cause her so much nervousness. She had a restlessness about her that wouldn't be quieted.

"No matter what, you know I'm here for you, right?" Vihaan said, trying to calm her down.

"Well, I guess that's good, all things considered. I may be testing that."

Vihaan heard the tremor of fear in her voice and had to control the urge to comfort her.

"I made a decision a couple of days ago. And that decision involves you. Maybe?"

Katherine got up and moved from the couch to the love seat. Then she turned to look him square in the face, and when she opened her mouth, nothing came out. She fell back on the love seat, giving a groan of disgust.

Again, he wanted to go to her to pull her into his embrace and tell her that whatever the problem was, he would help her. Whatever it was that Katherine was wrestling with, it didn't look like she wanted his help right now. She had made the decision that she had to ask him something, and whatever it was, she thought it was huge.

"I know I told you that in the past I've had some issues when it comes to putting colors together or doing other things that other women do when it comes to designing things, right?"

"Yeah, you said that you had some issues."

"Well, let me tell you about the biggest issue, and then we can go from there."

Vihaan was still lost, but he was going to wait until she got this all out.

"So the whole story is… Well, what I'm trying to say is… Oh, whatever. What I'm trying to say is I need your help, and I want you to teach me how to go ahead and design things in that kind of girly way. There, it's out."

Vihaan was panicking. This couldn't be happening. The woman who he wanted to have a family with and be with had asked him to be her boyfriend and teach her how to design things. He had to think. There had to be an answer to get them back on the right track.

When he didn't answer right away, Katherine stood up from the couch, throwing her hands in the air and saying she understood.

"I'm sorry, Vihaan. I should never have asked you. I mean, I'm not even sure that it's even possible to teach me that kind of thing."

With each word, it seemed to bring his dream closer to death. He had to do something; this just couldn't be the way it ended.

Vihaan stood up and went to Katherine. He placed his hands on her shoulders. He looked her in the eye, and he smiled.

"Katherine, there is no problem. Of course I can

teach this to you, but we do live in a small town. I want you to consider that I would be more than happy to teach you if we, in turn, could also look like we had just started dating."

"Dating! Why would we need to even do that?"

Vihaan took a step back and held his hands out. "It's not about you or me. It's about what it looks like to the town. The gossip mill is strong in Sweet Blooms. I want to make sure that you continue to get friends. And I also want to make sure that the women in the town don't think that I'm that kind of guy."

"What kind of guy would that be?"

"The one that takes a woman shopping and goes and looks at intimate apparel and different kinds of paint. The one that goes to various clothing stores and then says, 'oh, we are just friends.'"

"Do you really think we're going to have to do that?"

Vihaan nodded. "I do think we will have to do that, and remember, the whole dating thing isn't about you; it's about me The whole dating thing is to make sure that I can still make a family here in Sweet Blooms. Mothers will not be very eager for their daughters to date me when they will be able to point to us and say 'he's not ready to settle down. See how he acted with Katherine?'"

"Well, maybe this will help you with your problem too."

"My problem?"

"Yes, your problem. Everyone in town knows you, but if you're hoping to find a wife, we're gonna have to work on your image."

For a moment, Vihaan was offended.

"My image? I'm considerate and try to be kind to everyone. I make sure that I'm respectful to my elders. What is wrong with my image?"

"Everything you said is true, and that would be fine if you were looking to be someone's best friend or even someone's unofficial brother. But if you wanna make yourself look more like husband material, you are definitely gonna have to fix this image."

The irony was not lost on Vihaan. Here he was trying to get close to the woman that he was pretty sure was the one. And she wanted to help him with his image to look more like husband material. Suhana would roll when she heard this.

"So, you will help me look more husbandly?"

Katherine nodded. "Just a little more manly. Fortunately, you have all of the parts there; they're just not always working in the right way. But that's fine. That I can help you with if you can help me with mine."

Vihaan extended his hand. Katherine looked at it and smiled. She grabbed it and pumped it vigorously.

"Don't worry, Vihaan, you won't regret this."

Vihaan was already having second thoughts.

Six

"Didn't I tell you all roads lead back to Suhana?" Suhana said as she walked into Katherine's office. Suhana had a pixie grin on her face and a mischievous glint in her eye. "Like a good friend, you had only to call, and here I am. Now tell me, what has Vihaan done that you think you need to call me?"

Katherine had debated calling Suhana more than once. But who else could she tell about the deal she had made with Vihaan? She was short on friends, and she knew she was going to need some insider help.

"First, I have to ask you a question, Suhana."

"Ask away."

"I'm going to need your help, but I don't want to put you into an uncomfortable position. What I need to know is, are you gonna be okay keeping secrets?"

"Are we talking about female secrets?"

Katherine nodded her head.

"Then we have no problems. As long as there's nothing that's going to hurt Vihaan, your secrets are safe with me."

"I'm going out on the line here, but options are few."

"Wow, I hope you don't start every negotiation like

this; otherwise, I could see how people might think you're a little abrupt. Fortunately, I am made of sterner stuff, so it doesn't affect me at all. Continue."

The moment was at hand, and Katherine had called Suhana to help her. Now that everybody was where they were supposed to be, Katherine was fidgeting in her seat. Was this the right way? Now that she was getting ready to tell someone what had transpired between her and Vihaan, doubt clouded her mind. Suhana reached out and slammed both of her palms down on Katherine's desk. The sound jolted Katherine out of her reverie.

Suhana grabbed her head with both of her hands. "Please, please stop thinking so hard. I'm here. It's too late for me to go back. Besides, I am entirely too nosy to leave this office without hearing what happened between you and Vihaan."

"If you say it like that," Katherine mumbled. "Well, here goes."

Suhana scooted a little closer to the desk.

"Vihaan and I made an agreement on how we can help each other."

"Help each other?" Suhana said, confused.

Suhana had been to the house. In fact, Katherine could still remember her horrified look when she came into the house.

"Vihaan came to my apartment," Katherine said. "He must have seen what you saw, and he agreed that I needed some help."

Suhana nodded. "I didn't say you needed help; I just couldn't believe anyone was living in such a place. I could give you the names of some people who could go into your place and make it a vision to live in."

"If I can't do what he wants or if I find the tasks too hard, I may still do that," Katherine said. "But I agreed I would let him help me, and I would help him at the same time."

She held her hands up to stop Katherine from speaking. "I think I need to hear what exactly we are doing and not doing here. You keep saying the both of you have a problem, but I don't think you've said what his problem is."

Katherine cleared her throat and let out a big sigh before staring at Suhana. "Vihaan agreed to help me learn how to design and decorate with colors and stuff like other women. I, in return, said I would help him improve his image as a man."

Suhana had a confused looked on her face. Then five seconds passed and her hands went to her mouth. After that, she couldn't even contain herself in her seat. She got up and started laughing.

"You told Mr. Bachelor, Mr. I Can Make Money Like it Grows on Trees, that he wasn't manly enough? Why am I never in the room for these moments?"

Katherine raised her eyebrow as she watched Suhana pace. "I think you're not in the room because you'd probably act like this."

Katherine was so relieved that she wasn't laughing at her. She thought Suhana might say something to the effect of 'I've seen your apartment, there is no way that he can help you be more feminine.' Instead, she was harping on Vihaan.

"Well, that was certainly something," Suhana said as she took her seat. "So, is the reason you said yes to letting him show you how to design because you think he's not very manly?"

It was Katherine's turn to look confused. When she realized what Suhana was saying, she gasped. "Oh, no! I hope he didn't take it that way." She moaned.

"Then directly after you asked him to help you do something girly, you told him he's not very manly. I'm not sure what else he could have thought," Suhana said through barely concealed laughs.

"It can't be. I explained!"

"Oh, this I have got to hear."

"I told him he was attractive, kind, and considerate, but he just came off as a great brother to have, not a man you want to have sweep you away." Katherine's voice went lower and lower as she heard the words that she was saying. "That's why I called you. I needed to bounce this off of someone else. Maybe I acted rashly or too soon, or I don't know, but there is still time for me to go back to him and call it off."

"Hold on. I think a lot of things should happen here, but calling it off isn't one of them," Suhana said. "I think that you and Vihaan are very smart people. Smart people always find the most complicated way to do the most simple things. So, hearing this arrangement is not surprising. Entertaining, maybe, but not surprising. You do know that you and Vihaan have the same problem?"

Katherine wanted to pretend she didn't have a clue, but she was honest, and always with herself. "Yes, I do know what our problem is. It's about caring what other people think. It's about hoping that someone else will sign off on us."

Suhana smiled. "You are way smarter than Vihaan is. I'm glad that means I don't really have to interfere in this at all. I can just sit back and see how it all plays out as long as I know one of you understands what the issue is. I know you'll both figure it out."

"You have a lot of faith in both of us. But I will say that he took it really well about the whole thing. He didn't argue with me. He didn't laugh at me. I was really scared about what was going to happen, and I have to say he made it all really comfortable for me."

Suhana smiled. "You talk like a woman who's interested in a man, not like a woman who was speaking about the good qualities of her brother."

"Listen, I'm not saying he doesn't have attractive qualities. Let's be honest; he looks amazing! And if you looked at each one of his characteristics, it seems like they should all make one of the world's sexiest men. Instead, when you see all of them together, he becomes the best Boy Scout ever."

Suhana laughed. "Boy Scout, huh?"

Katherine waved off her laughter. "You know what I mean."

"Okay, so how are you two masterminds going to perform this feat in the little town of *I'm in your business for your own good* Sweet Blooms?"

Katherine smiled. "Vihaan had a plan for that."

"Oh, I just bet he did. What was this masterful plot?"

"We're going to be dating. That way, the townspeople won't think I'm corrupting him with my evil city ways, and he will be able to find a woman later."

Suhana clapped. "Geniuses."

Katherine gave her a lopsided grin. "I have to tell you, Suhana, I feel like you're laughing at me and not with me."

Suhana stood up. "Well, we must go to the spa."

"Spa? It's morning, and I haven't got any work done yet."

"Work will always be there. I have to tell you that one of the things you need to remember is how you look can affect how you feel. Once you come out of the spa, you will feel pampered, delicate, and beautiful. That will help in the long run."

Katherine looked at Suhana suspiciously. "How I look will help me pick better designs and match colors?"

"No, but if you look good, people try to see the beauty in what you pick more."

Suhana shrugged, and Katherine laughed. "I'm glad I called you, Suhana."

With a delicate eyebrow raised, she said, "Most people see the light after they call me. Now come on, we have to get in the spa, and it's short notice for a day."

Katherine discovered that beauty is a beast. On the day that she went to the spa, Vihaan called out to say he would be gone for the next two days to scout materials. When she was at the spa, they not only worked over her whole body, but the stylist had new ideas for her hair. By the time everyone was done, Katherine had a regimen that she had to do every day. It seemed like it took longer to do the regimen than it did to get dressed.

Two days later, she was standing on her porch with a bonsai tree. She was snipping off pieces of the tree, looking for its inner shape and her inner peace. Her hair was piled on top of her head. The stylist said it made her neck look longer. She wasn't sure what her neck looked like, but she was sure there was sweat running down it. She also had to wear these silly gloves to hold really small scissors in order to snip the bonsai. Suhana assured her after she got her nails done that she should be wearing gloves everywhere to protect the color.

Then his truck pulled into the driveway. While she was trying to look delicate and fresh, he stepped out of his no doubt air-conditioned truck and walked towards her just like one of those models in a jeans commercial where no one knows what's being advertised. The wind was ruffling his hair. The breeze plastered his vee neck t-shirt to his muscled chest. It was all part of a production, and then he spoke. "It appears you need some help trimming that tree."

Katherine looked at him and cocked her head to the side. "How could you have messed that up? You had it all going there, and then…"

Vihaan had a confused look. "What happened?"

"You were the perfect moving commercial of manhood coming to rescue me, and I wanted to hear you say something like 'can I help you?' or even something corny like 'looks like all the flowers are out today.'"

A grin flashed across his face. "You're not a morning person, are you?" he asked.

"First, the morning was over at ten. Second, it's almost three. I thought if I came out here after noon, I'd beat the worst of the heat."

"If it's any consolation, you were right; it's not as hot now."

Katherine tossed her gloves and the scissors down. "I'm done being delicate in this sun. Come on in. This was all for your benefit anyway."

"My benefit?"

"Yeah, it was, but it's not working for me, so..." Katherine looked at him with her arms crossed over her chest. She was tired, and she felt dumb. There was nothing worse to her than feeling dumb. "You're back. Why did you come by?"

"I came by to get started. To do that, I needed to look at your place and clothing," he said, walking into the house.

She thought they were going into the living room. She was wrong. He went through the living room and into her bedroom. She didn't rush ahead of him; she knew what he would find.

Her bed was covered with a quilt with a big flower on it. Her bed was made. Her slippers were in front of her bed. Her dresser had all of her toiletries in a row on top of it. There was also a small desk in the room. That desk had a small desk lamp in the upper left-hand corner, her laptop, which was in the middle of the desk, and her chair, which had a throw blanket on the back of it just in case she got cold and didn't want to break her workflow to get a blanket.

She knew what was in there and expected him to come right out and give her a commentary. Instead, she waited, and he stayed inside. After two minutes, she went in. She wasn't sure what she was expecting, but it wasn't him staring into her closet.

Katherine walked into her bedroom and stood behind him.

"What's wrong?"

He turned and looked at her, and then turned to look back at the closet.

"You don't see the problem, Katherine?"

Katherine looked into the closet, trying to see what it was that he was seeing. Inside the closet was all of her work clothes. She had five pairs of black pants, followed by ten white shirts, followed by five jackets, and all of them were black. There was a garment bag in that closet as well. The garment bag was red. Katherine knew inside of the bag was a blue suit with a beige top. All of it looked in order.

"No, Vihaan, I don't see the problem at all."

He held out his hand, and Katherine put hers in his. Then he pulled her along, and they left her bedroom and went into the kitchen. Katherine knew something was wrong, but what it was she couldn't pinpoint. When he arrived in her kitchen, she let out a sigh. The kitchen was the way it was, and some people thought it looked nice. When Katherine had gone looking for a home, the realtor thought the kitchen was the biggest selling point. It turned out the fact it was on a block with quiet or no neighbors was more important to her.

She sat down at the pedestal kitchen table and waited for Vihaan to speak. She knew it weighed on him because he was pacing back and forth. When she was about to get up and make some coffee, he held his hands out to stop her.

"Sit, please. I need to get my thoughts together."

Katherine sat down, and then she waited for him to settle.

"Vihaan, you need to speak because you are making me nervous."

He looked at her and then took a seat.

"Do you have non-work clothes?"

Katherine laughed. "Of course I do. Did you think

those were my only clothes? No, I have two pairs of jeans and eight recreational tops."

"Recreational tops? That is the first time I've heard that one."

Katherine recognized that tone. It was the *she had done something that wasn't expected* tone. "What did I do now?" She got up and started to make some coffee. She made cups for both of them to settle her nerves.

"I don't think it's about what you did. I think I was surprised to see you were so organized."

Katherine was okay with that.

"What are you saying? That when I learn how to design things, I won't be organized anymore?"

"Well, let's just say I'd like to see you arrange your closet the way you have it in there with your new talent."

"What are we saying, that women who know how to design don't know how to organize?"

"No, I'm not saying that at all. What I am saying is that when you have more clothes and more color options, organizing becomes a little more of a challenge."

"If you have more clothes, you don't have a plan. So I don't think I need to worry about getting more clothes because my plan used to work with the clothes that you see in that closet."

"Before we begin, I want to make sure I understand what your thoughts are about certain colors."

" Okay."

"I'm going to say a color, and I want you to tell me the first thing that comes into your mind."

Katherine nodded.

"Pink."

"Barbie."

"Red."

"Woman in Red."

"White."

"Marilyn Monroe."

"Blue."

"Smarts and college."

"Black."

"Stability."

When they were done, she could see Vihaan looking at her as if he were trying to figure out a huge puzzle. Then he smiled and nodded.

"What? Did you find what you were looking for?"

"I did. So now I know how to start and what to do."

Katherine smiled. "So we can do this today?"

"We can start."

"Start? Don't you have some charts or things I can study?"

"No, Katherine, that's not how we are going to do this. I promise you will have notes, homework, and something tangible."

Katherine nodded, feeling a little better."

Vihaan stood up. "Your homework is to pick two colors and think about how they make you feel. You can look at them online and in books and other places, but look around and write down how they make you feel. I will create a schedule, and that way, you'll feel comfortable when we are doing things. There is no book because this is going to be your personal style."

Katherine nodded. She wasn't so sure what any color could make her feel, but she would give it a try. She followed him to the door. He turned and stepped towards her. Katherine thought he forgot something and stepped back as well.

"Did you forget something? I can—" When she saw him shake his head, she was confused for a moment, and then it came to her.

"Vihaan, did you want to kiss me?"

He put his hands in his pockets and nodded.

Katherine looked at him and smiled. "You see this whole body language here? It says you need to be in the friend zone."

Vihaan's expression looked uncomfortable and bordering on distressed. Katherine thought it was time to do her part.

"There are several problems with the kiss that didn't happen. The first thing is you didn't prepare me, and I don't feel all that confident with you."

"You don't feel confident?"

"No. So when I say I don't feel confident, it doesn't mean I want you to go out and do something amazing; it just means that when I'm around you, I want to know that you are able to take care of anything that comes up. Not that I'm expecting anything to come up, but if it happens, I just wanna make sure I'm not the one who needs to go and fight the mugger."

"So, you don't feel safe?"

"Safe is a strong word today. What I want to do is, I want to make sure that you are confident with you." Katherine could see that Vihaan still looked confused. "What I'm trying to say is this: I don't want a mindless caveman. But I do wanna make sure if a prehistoric animal should jump out and try to attack us that you will jump out in front of me and try to save me."

Vihaan looked at her and shook his head. "You must know that makes no sense."

Katherine held up her hand. "One, of course it makes sense because you want to kiss me. So just about all things I say make sense. Two, this is a journey for you to go on. It will make you more attentive to me, and I will appreciate you more because you are willing to try to be more attentive to me."

Vihaan laughed. "Suhana is right. It's the women who have the power."

Katherine laughed. "I like Suhana. She's a wise woman."

Seven

"Vihaan."

Vihaan put his pen down and sat back in his chair. Hearing his aunt Anika wasn't a surprise; he just wasn't sure when she would show up.

"Auntie."

Anika walked into his office and took a seat. She was dressed in blue jeans and a yellow top. Whatever she wanted, she really wanted him to agree to because she had worn jeans and a top. She preferred to wear dresses, but when she wanted to appear more modern, she wore jeans.

Anika was close to, if not, seventy. She was small but heavyset. At five foot five, she had long black hair that she kept in a knot on her head. With almond eyes framed by laugh lines that showed she had lived a happy life and smooth mocha skin, she was still an attractive woman.

When she sat down in the chair, Vihaan prepared himself for a conversation that would run around the block before the point was made.

Anika brought out a package from her purse. He could smell the fresh bread from where he sat. Oh, he didn't know what the question was, but it was big.

"I bring a gift, yet I don't get a hug?"

Vihaan smiled. "I don't know how much that bread is."

Anika waved him off. "I can't come and visit?"

"Of course you can; not that you've ever done that, but you always could."

"Well, I've decided it is a good time. We don't talk, and sometimes things get lost."

"Things like?"

"Like I'm sure it was just an oversight that you didn't return Anum's phone call."

Then it became clear what the visit was about. Anum was the daughter of a friend of Anika's. He had spoken to Anum who apologized for both women, saying everyone was concerned she was never going to marry and so a flock of men had been found to parade in front of her.

"I spoke to Anum. She is very nice, but I am not looking, and neither is she."

Anika sighed in exasperation. "Everyone is looking until they find someone. All of you kids say you don't want anyone, but then one day you show up married. You know what that is? Looking until you find someone."

Vihaan smiled and reached for the bread. He knew the rest was coming. This was the run around the park.

"It was a big shock that you were not going to take the jobs in the city."

"I can see that," he said around the bread.

"The money is good, and it would make getting married much easier. Everyone wants to be with someone who is stable. But we still have options. You can go back and take the jobs, or you can start looking for a wife."

"Why do I need to do one or the other?"

Anika tsked at him. "Vihaan, you are almost forty. You're getting old. You need to be young enough to run around with your children, or you need to have enough money to pay someone else to run around with your children."

Vihaan almost choked on the last of the bread. "I can see your point, but right now I don't need you to set up any more dates for me. I think I can find a woman if I want one."

"There is some town gossip going around that you spend a lot of time with the woman you work with. I told my friend it was gossip because you wouldn't think about being with a woman no matter where she is from and not bring her home first, right?"

So we finally have gotten to the core of the visit.

"I think that I'm old enough to make decisions on my own. I've dated without my family's say so in the past, and I may do so in the future."

"We are your family."

"I know. I love you, and I appreciate you, but at the end of the day, it's me who has to live with me, not you. I need to be able to face myself in the mirror."

Anika looked at him, stunned. "I can see you are busy, so I'm going to leave you now. Think on Anum. I know you both say you are not looking, but until you are married, everyone is looking."

Anika left, and a few minutes later, he heard a rapping on his door.

"Come in."

Katherine came in and looked at him. Then she went around his desk to stand in front of him.

"Katherine?"

She reached down placed her hands on both sides of his face, then leaned down and placed a light kiss on one side of his mouth. She placed another small kiss on the other side of his mouth. The kiss didn't linger but was sweet and quick.

When she stood up, Vihaan grabbed her hands before she could leave.

"What was that for?"

"These walls are as thin as paper. I came in while you were in the middle of the conversation. I can now say after hearing from you with her, I think if a prehistoric beast came, you'd throw your body in front of mine," she said and then left him smiling in his office.

"Hello auntie," Suhana said as her aunt Anika walked in. She knew this visit was coming. She didn't know when she would come, but she did know it was coming.

"Suhana."

If there was a way to have a tone of disapproval, Anika had it for Suhana. Suhana kept the smile on her face and stepped aside as her aunt walked into her studio apartment. She didn't expect any pleasantries, and she didn't get any. This wasn't the way it had always been. Once Suhana had lived in a house. Once Suhana had been in love.

Today she was a living testament of that love and beacon of hope for other members in her family who wanted love but weren't sure how it all worked.

It was a shame that Anika didn't see her that way.

Anika walked into the flat, and Suhana saw her take a look at the walls decorated with pictures of Suhana and Zachary. Some of them were single pictures, but most of them were joint pictures. Zachary was as pale as Suhana was brown. He had blonde hair and blue eyes. He was a gift to Suhana and a pain in the side to Anika.

Suhana closed the door and waited. She wanted to see what approach Anika was going to take today. Anika walked along the walls as if seeing the pictures for the first time. The wait was part of the game. Suhana knew the rules, and still, she was antsy waiting for Anika to began.

"I'm sure you're wondering why I came here today," Anika said, walking to the middle of the room. "We don't speak often, and when we do speak, it doesn't seem to be the most pleasant occurrence. You're standing at the door. Won't you offer an old woman some tea?"

Suhana locked the door and then went into the dine-in kitchen. On the counter, she had a teapot in a tea warmer. She poured the tea and placed it as an invitation on the small table that doubled as a desk.

"Auntie, please have some tea. Things are good in my life."

"We both know I'm not here for you, Suhana. You are a lost cause that I can only hope one day realizes her mistakes and owns up to them."

Suhana had to clench her teeth against the response she wanted to make. Instead, she looked Anika in the eye and continued as if nothing had affected her.

"Then why ware you here? I know I'm not on the way to anywhere."

Anika took a sip of the tea and then took another look around the studio. Her gaze came to rest on a picture on the table. It was a heart shaped picture frame of Suhana and Zachary.

"Family is important to me, Suhana," she said and then took another sip. "It gives me purpose and reassures me that the customs and ways we have today will be taught to the children of tomorrow. Those things aren't easy to keep, and sometimes they come at a price."

"We all have to decide if the price is too high, Anika."

"You would think that. Things must have a priority. First must come duty and then will come love." Anika took another sip of tea.

"I'm sure by now you've met the woman Vihaan works with. What did you think of her?"

"I think she's an honest woman."

Anika nodded. "Her honesty isn't in question. Did you think she was a good woman to fit into our family and carry on our traditions?"

Suhana wrapped her hands around her teacup and tried to stay in the present time and place. These words were the same words she had heard when Zachary was alive.

"I think her value has to be determined by Vihaan. None of us can play matchmaker in this day and age." Finishing the rest of her tea, Suhana got up and put her cup in the sink.

Anika pushed her cup away.

"You're not going to wash that dish? You know a good woman keeps an empty sink."

Suhana pushed away from the sink and sat down at the table with Anika.

"We both know I am long past being a good woman."

Anika looked at the picture frame. "It's not always about you, Suhana. You should think of Vihaan. Think about if you want him to be alone like you are."

Suhana looked at the frame, and she saw Zachary's face smiling at her. He had been the love of her life. She had been working as a waitress, and he had met her during the lunch rush. He had given her the standard line about how beautiful she was, and he had told her she wasn't the most beautiful woman he had ever met, but she was the first woman that made him take a second look and think about what their children would look like.

He had been outrageous, bold, and he embraced life with all that he had. He didn't believe in cutting corners or hoping tomorrow would be a better day. With him, they had traveled, camped, and seen all of the United States before they found out that he had cancer. When they weren't sure how much time they would have, Suhana had begged him to think about children.

Zachary had said no. He said he wouldn't leave her alone to raise a child with no family. His family hadn't been welcoming and had blamed her for taking him away during his last months. Suhana's family had been distant, and Anika had been rude.

When Zachary died, he had made her promise to forgive her family. That they had those views because they had never known love. If they had, they'd know how precious a gift it was between them.

Suhana pointed to the picture. "Do you see Zachary in that photo? He's happy," Suhana said.

Anika nodded in agreement. "Yes, he was, but his happiness cost too much," Anika snapped back. "His happiness cost a mother her chance to say goodbye to her son. His happiness caused you to turn your back on your family. Duty first and then love."

Suhana blinked back tears of acknowledgment. She

knew all the arguments. She and Anika had gone back and forth with Anika being a master of guilting her into believing her love had cost Zachary's family the most.

"So what happens when love comes first and it doesn't agree with duty?" she whispered.

Anika stood up.

"Do you think you are the only one on the planet to ever love? To know the bloom and wonder of love and then be told you can't keep it. I know what you think. You think I was cruel to begrudge your time with Zachary. Yes, I remember his name. When you found out he was sick, then it became even more important to you to spend time with him.

I just want you to know that true love sacrifices. It looks beyond itself and does what is right for the other person. Zachary has been gone for two years. Your apartment is a shrine to him and what was.

You are bold, brash, and vibrant to the world, but you come back to this tomb to reminisce over what was and what will never be. You say this is love and I say it's not. We don't have to agree on this, Suhana. In fact, we never will, but think of Vihaan.

Will you put him on the road of being alone with Katherine? Are you willing to risk his life turning out like this?"

Suhana heard the words, and they were like daggers in her soul. Her words weren't new; in fact, if Suhana was honest, she had heard these words from herself. Hearing them a second time didn't lessen the impact of them.

"What do you want from me, auntie?" she asked in a low, pained voice.

"I want you to look at Vihaan and this woman and see the truth of how things will be. Don't see them and imagine this is the second chance for you and Zachary. Think on it and then do what your love for Vihaan says you should do."

With that, Anika turned and let herself out. Suhana walked to her futon and laid down. She couldn't see the futon by the time she got to it. Her feet went there out of memory.

Her mind went back to her and Zachary. She pulled the pillow on the futon into her embrace. Zachary had bought the pillow. On one side, the pillow said Live True, and the other side said Play Hard. She had tried to do what it was that Zachary had asked. Moving on was harder than she thought.

Everyone had said that time would make it easier, but time made her more desperate. She curled up tighter with the pillow and let her silent tears flow. Her pain was still so deep that when she cried, only a gasp of air escaped.

She dug her hands into the pillow and let Anika's words swallow her. She was living in a tomb. She might argue a pretty tomb, but it was a tomb nonetheless. She had caught glimpses of what it was, but she couldn't bring herself to let go of the memories she had of Zachary. Every time she couldn't remember his face at a place they had gone, she had put up another picture of them.

Vihaan had a chance. Suhana just needed to make sure she was helping him with his chance or trying to make sure she could see the future of her and Zachary in someone else.

<h1 style="text-align:center">*Eight*</h1>

It was late afternoon, and Katherine and Vihaan were sitting at the table in the makeshift kitchen in the office. They had been going over budgets for the community center all day long.

"I don't know what I can buy on this budget," Vihaan murmured.

"You can buy what you need," quipped Katherine.

"I usually have a larger, freer budget when I'm working on something where concept and vision are a pivotal piece," he said.

"Well, it must be nice when people make allowances for creativity and genius," she mumbled.

"It has its advantages. It gives you the freedom to be."

Katherine looked at him. "Do you feel like I'm hemming you in? That you can't do what it is that you need to?"

He lifted his head up as if he were just hearing her.

"I'm not complaining about the company. I'm just saying I'm trying to understand my options."

"Oh, that's fine. I thought you were feeling trapped working with someone who wasn't as creatively endowed as you were."

"Dating, by the way."

"What?"

"I'm not just working with you; remember, we are dating."

"Ah, so you say."

With that, Vihaan looked up with a furrowed brow. "What is that supposed to mean?"

"It means we need to work on that if you think we are dating. You were doing so good the other day, and now you are back to the friend zone. I think you need rules."

"Rules?"

"Yes. Don't be upset. I think rules are great, and they keep us on track."

"Rules on how to date?"

"No, rules on keeping you out of the friend zone. So what you need are the twelve steps of intimacy, and if you practice these, we should be fine."

"Twelve steps? Like twelve steps Alcoholics Anonymous? And twelve steps to…"

"Yes! Now listen. There are twelve steps. I think if you start there, you will be out of the friend zone."

"Okay, tell me."

"Step one, you have to look at me, all of me, so I know you might be interested. You've got that."

Vihaan threw up his hands. "At least you noticed that."

Katherine smiled. "Step two, we have to have eye to eye contact. You know those moments when our eyes meet and we know we are both interested?"

"Hold on. If I look at you like this, you ask me what's wrong. How is this going to be romantic?"

Katherine blew out a breath.

"I will not get distressed if you look at me the right way."

Vihaan laughed. "So I'm so supposed to look at you the right way? I look at you my way and you ask what's wrong. I'm supposed to know what the right way is?"

"It's a rule, yes!"

Vihaan held up both of his hands. "Okay, let's just say I'm looking at you the right way. I told you, you're beautiful, and you know I'm interested."

Katherine stopped.

"You didn't say I was beautiful, by the way."

Vihaan smiled. "I'm sure I did, but this step I can do. Katherine, you are most definitely beautiful."

Katherine smiled at Vihaan. "Thank you."

They looked into each other's eyes and leaned across the table. When he met her halfway, she spoke.

"That's the look I'm talking about."

Vihaan reached out and tucked her hair behind her ear. Katherine smiled and spoke in a low voice.

"You've skipped a couple of steps."

He continued to touch her hair. "I'm a very avant person. I don't always follow the rules, but I can guarantee the end will be something everyone wants."

"The next steps are talking, and then step eight is hand to face."

"The steps need a little reorganization."

Vihaan leaned forward some more and rested his forehead against hers. "I don't know the steps you are talking about, but one of the steps for me is sharing breath."

Katherine looked him in the eye.

"This, Katherine, is one of the more personal things that can be done between two people. It means I trust you. I want to be around you, and most of all, it allows each person to walk away with a little piece of the other person."

Katherine nodded.

Vihaan smiled. "I think I'm going to love doing these steps of intimacy."

Suhana had been to Vihaan's office more than her fair share. She knew everything about the Cade ranch. She liked to come in the early hours when nature was just waking up. The bigger thrill for her was watching Vihaan work. He was truly was the best of them all wrapped up in one.

Standing in front of the building, she was plagued with second thoughts. She knew Vihaan was there because she saw the monster truck that he called his little baby. Remembering when they went to buy the truck brought a smile to her face. Vihaan had told her he needed a truck that said *look at me.* She had pointed him towards all the small European cars, and he had given them a once over but hadn't been moved. When he saw the truck, he said he had found his true love. When she mentioned that he now had a truck like everyone else in Sweet Blooms, he told her the truck wasn't to get noticed in Sweet Blooms, it was to get noticed in the city.

Zachary had loved trucks. She hadn't been able to keep his. It was too many memories. Memories. That's what had brought her here today. Anika was right. She was alone. She didn't want that same fate for Vihaan.

Taking a deep breath, she continued and opened up

the building door. Inside there was a rustling of paper. She looked around, hoping to see Vihaan walking about. One moment she was alone in the hallway, and the next moment, Vihaan came blindly walking out of his office. He was shuffling papers and trying to figure out how to keep them in his grip.

"Vihaan," Suhana called out. His head popped up, and for a moment, he was confused, and then he smiled.

"What are you doing here, troublemaker?"

"I came to talk to the famous architect designer. Maybe he is too famous to talk to his lowly family," she jested.

His grin widened. "Normally, I would take the time to take you to task, but today I am already late for a meeting."

"I can wait—"

Vihaan shook his head as he finally balanced the tubes in his arms. "No, no, I won't be back for a while. It's offsite, not here. Ms. Waters had a vision last night, and I have to see if it fits in with mine and with the budget Katherine gave me. So I'm sorry, but not today."

Vihaan shuffled past her, and the only thing she could do was follow behind him.

"Call me tonight, and we will plan for tomorrow," he said. Suhana nodded and watched him ride away. Disheartened at her failed attempt, she thought about waiting for him in town. She got in her car and drove into town. She found parking in front of Sweet Blooms. She had been so sure about coming to wait for him, but even now, she was undecided. Maybe a sweet or two would help her pass the time.

She bought two cupcakes and then went to stand by her car. This was a first; the smell of pastries wafted under her nose, but she wasn't inclined to eat them at all. She was contemplating who she could give the pastries to so it wouldn't be a waste. Maybe a stop by the diner to give to Aunt Geeta. If she did, she would have to explain what she was doing in town in the first place, and she didn't want to start the inevitable war that would happen between Anika and Aunt Geeta.

Suhana heard the steady clip of shoes and saw Clarissa was approaching. Clarissa, the town beauty queen and, according to some, the woman who was always looking for a significant other who also had money. If the town gossip was to be believed, that is. If Suhana had to guess, she'd say that Clarissa was in her thirties. It looked like she had changed her hair color because now they were dark auburn tresses that danced around her shoulders. She was dressed in a strapless red and white polka dot dress that hugged her curves and was offset by matching red heels.

Suhana wiggled her toes in her sandals. She couldn't imagine walking in heels in sunny weather much less the ones Clarissa had on.

"Hello, Suhana. Life must be pretty sad if you are standing with a Sweet Blooms box in your hand and you're still looking lost. At the very least, you should be eating them."

Suhana looked at the box and then at Clarissa. There was nothing to say. She was right.

"I'm going to have coffee at the new shop. Do you want to come with me? My treat?"

"Well," Suhana said, trying to conjure up a reason why she couldn't go with Clarissa. Then she thought about it. She should go. It would give her a reason to hang around and wait for Vihaan if nothing else.

Besides, she wasn't sure she really wanted to be by herself now anyway. "I think I will take you up on that."

Suhana brought the box with her. If they were going to have coffee, then the pastries wouldn't go to waste. Once they got there, they were immediately seated. The waitress took the order, and Clarissa extended her long legs out. Suhana couldn't resist.

"How do you walk all day in those?"

Clarissa smiled. "Because I have to." Suhana expected a lot of answers, but that wasn't one of them. The waitress delivered the drinks, and Clarissa began.

"Suhana, you are related to Vihaan the boy scout architect-designer who's making a name for himself."

Sunhana stopped, not sure what surprised her more—that she knew Vihaan or that she knew what he did for a living. The rumor was she knew all things when it came to money and men. Was she doing early reconnaissance on Vihaan?

"I didn't know that anyone in Sweet Blooms followed architecture," Suhana replied.

"I'm on the board. We track all of the contractors for the town. Adam Cade gave his name as a contractor."

"Oh."

"No, Suhana, I'm not looking to find out if he needs a wife. From what I hear, he has finally decided to try and get one."

Without even asking, Clarissa reached for the Sweet Blooms box and opened it up. She peered inside and smiled. "Carrot, I love carrot." After that exclamation, she pulled out the cupcake, peeled back the wrapper, and began to eat. When Suhana looked at her with an open mouth, Clarissa pushed the box towards her. "Eat up, there's one left."

"Vihaan hasn't made a firm decision on his choice of a wife yet," Suhana said as she picked up the other cupcake. "He's young, and I'm sure when he understands all of the ramifications of his choices, he may expand his search."

"I would have never thought you would be one of those people who let themselves be governed by rules and traditions."

"I love my family like everyone else. Sometimes that's all you have left."

"Family," Clarissa said. "They are the best and the worst. They know all of your weaknesses, and they use them ruthlessly when they need you to do something."

"Relationships are always a two-way street," Suhana interjected.

"So you've come to tell Vihaan to look someplace else for happiness?"

"Why do you even care one way or the other?" Suhana fired back.

"Let's say I'm more observant than caring. Your aunt Anika came into town. She was looking for Vihaan. She is a very focused woman. When we meet in town, if she can't cross the street before we pass one anoher, she makes sure to give me a disapproving stare."

Suhana knew the look. No matter what anyone thought about Clarissa, she was surprised Anika would be so openly rude.

Clarissa waved it off. "It's of no account. She had an unhappy look, and a *woman on a mission* look. Then, when she came back two hours later, I saw her as I was leaving Banter House. She had a small smile on her face. It's my experience that that means someone else is not a happy camper. Then I find you outside the holy ground of sugar rushes, and you're stuck by your car. This tells me that Anika wanted something from Vihaan. She probably tried to use a strong arm technique on him and it didn't work. So her next best thing is a soft whip. That would be you, Suhana. I'm just wondering if you are going to do it or not?"

Suhana looked at Clarissa. "I didn't know you—"

"That I could think? Keep it to yourself. I don't want the word to get around. Don't look so horrified. I just wanted to tell you to be careful what you do in the name of family. Sometimes people in our families don't like seeing other people breaking away. They think they are losing people when really they're gaining family as long as they're open."

"Clarissa, have you—"

Clarissa waved her finger in the air. "This isn't *let's ask Clarissa twenty questions.* This is about me seeing you looking lost, and normally you are bouncing around more than a flea in tall grass."

Suhana smiled. "Thank you, Clarissa. I need to go and talk to someone, but I want to thank you."

"Don't thank me. I'm not that old yet."

Suhana left her drink and the box on the table. She got up and walked toward Banter House. She found a little pep in her step again. She needed to do what she could live with. She was going to speak with Aunt Geeta, and then she'd keep on the course that she was already on.

Nine

Katherine was sitting at her desk trying to go over the new numbers Vihaan had submitted for his vision. She never knew vision was so expensive. In an attempt to minimize the cost, she had put out a request for proposal to several in-town vendors on how he could get his work done.

Since she'd put it out, she had received several visits from local vendors. They had come in with gifts . So far, she had gift baskets, coupons, and a promise of a knitted sweater by someone's grandmother.

When she heard the door open, she thought it was someone else bearing gifts.

"I'm not open for now. If you want to meet, please make an appointment." When she looked around down the hall, she saw it was Vihaan standing there with a smile. He had on blue jeans and a short sleeve shirt. There it was again, the commercial. He was smiling, walking down the hall, and then he was at her door.

"I've been looking for you."

Oh yeah, he was a quick study. She knew the smile on her face told him he had done his entrance right. This was the perfect approach. It was like watching a lion take a walk down the runway. It was the culmination of angles and lines that promised to deliver power and strength.

"I haven't been hiding. In fact, I think that's the problem."

"Every time I came in today, there were people beating me to the door. I think at one point there was an older woman who was giving me a dirty look. What's even worse is I think I know her from the matrons in the church."

Katherine laughed. "Why were you looking for me?"

"I wanted us to get together. You have been so diligent in keeping up your end of the bargain, I wanted to make sure I wasn't slacking."

"You?"

"I know, but I want to make sure you have all of my attention."

Katherine looked at him and hoped her mouth wasn't hanging open.

"All of your attention?"

"I can see you are overthinking every word I'm saying. I want you to relax. This will be like second nature to you by the time we're done."

"Really? And how can you be so sure?"

"Because I know you are a passionate woman with deep convictions. That means you have the ability to design and express those passions, unlike other women."

Katherine didn't know who he saw, but she sure hoped she could be that woman. She folded her hands so they wouldn't fidget.

"When did you plan on this gathering? And how much time will it take? Time is money, and we are in the middle of a project."

He came into her office and took a seat. "You want

to know how long what will take, the meeting or the unveiling of your true nature?"

She swallowed and looked at him sitting across her desk. Her breath came a little quicker. Was this Vihaan? He had been studying and taking her tips to heart. The man sitting across the desk from her couldn't be confused as anyone's brother. Trying to break the moment, Katherine waved him away.

"The meeting, of course."

He sat forward and leaned on her desk. "It's all up to you, Katherine. I'll let you set the pace."

"Okay, Mr. I'm the Fireman of Intimacy, hold your horses, and put away your hoses."

"I'm doing what you want me to do, and still I'm getting grief. I think you're rigging the system."

She scoffed at him. "We're at work. We shouldn't even be discussing this here. What if one of the many people walked in and heard us doing, you know, this."

He grinned, waving his hands, trying to imitate her movements. "I'm not sure what this is, but I agree this isn't the place. How about we work from home tomorrow, and I'll come by, and we can start fresh then."

"Did I need to get anything?"

"No, I'll bring what we need." With that, he got up and walked out of her office. When she heard his door close, she got up and closed hers as well. Then she went back to her desk and dropped her head on it.

What had she been thinking when she had said yes to this? The fact of the matter was that if he found a way to find this magical nature of hers, it would never compare with the emerging stud Vihaan was becoming. She had thrown out the gauntlet but hadn't really considered the ramifications.

She was about to have the town's most eligible bachelor show her how to be more in tune with her feminine side. That seemed like a no starter, but she had entered into the agreement eyes wide open. She wasn't intimidated by people because she could always fall back on her work. Now she had double dared someone who thrived on dares and challenges.

Okay, this might not have been her best move.

She had gone through all the options. She wasn't sure until she heard Vihaan leave the office. It was almost as if the slamming of the door was the solidification of her thoughts. She was going to have to tell Vihaan that this was a no go. He was already sexy, he had money, and she didn't need to know that feminine design stuff anyway. Yup, it had sounded great in her head, but she just had a suspicion that it wasn't going to go that well with Vihaan.

Vihaan stood in front of the door with four two-foot bolts of cloth. He rang the doorbell and waited for her to come. She had been scared the other day, and he wondered if she would try to find a way out of it today.

When she opened the door, she appeared tired. He hoped he wasn't the reason. Her hair was piled on top of her head, and she had on a grey workout half shirt that said 'Yes I can!' All that was topped off by black yoga pants that outlined her shape, showcasing her muscular thighs.

"I'm just finishing up my yoga," she said.

"I won't bother you. I'll go in the living room," he said, walking in as she stepped aside.

She smiled. "You've obviously mistaken my place for somewhere that has space."

"When there's no color, the perspective can be off."

"Is that what you tell the girls to get into their place?" she joked.

He turned to face her and smiled. "I don't usually have to tell them anything to get into their home."

She leaned against the wall and then looked at him.

"We need to talk."

"No good conversation starts with those words. Tell me, what is the problem?"

"There's no problem. I just can't do this."

He held up the bolts of cloth in his arms. "You can't look at these? Is the color too strong?"

She let out a breath for patience. "No, the colors are amazing and vibrant. It's the you helping me, me helping you in that man-woman thingy."

Vihaan gripped the bolts tighter. H wasn't expecting this. He had to think quickly.

"Why can't you do this now?"

"Well, it's because you don't really need any help at all."

He was thrilled and scared all at once. She was seeing him different, but it was driving her away?

"Help me out here, Katherine. Why don't you want me to help you?"

"Because it won't work. The exchange wouldn't be right."

He put down the bolts of cloth and then turned to her. She hadn't really had time to look at him, but he had on a grey shirt and black jeans. He took in a breath and tried to keep his thoughts logical.

"I'm not wanting to offend you, but why won't it work? Is it because I'm part Indian?"

She crossed her hands over her chest, unwittingly pushing it up as if she were putting her chest on a platter. She shifted her weight and tapped her foot in annoyance. "No, stop the foolishness. More importantly, stop fishing for compliments. You've seen yourself. You don't need any help from the likes of me. What was I thinking to help you be more manly? I'm still trying to get the girly part down. No, I'm thinking I should do this with someone who is as lost as I am so it'll be an even game."

He internally calmed down. He knew she was reserved, so he had expected this to happen sooner. "So what are you saying, you think I'm not man enough to make decisions about what is feminine?"

He saw her look at him, and for a moment she was speechless.

"You really want to have a discussion about this?!"

He stepped closer and placed his hands on her shoulder. "I found your steps of intimacy, and one of them is hands to shoulder. It means I don't mind people seeing that I'm interested in you. Do you think I'd do that with a woman who wasn't very feminine?"

Her eyes half closed as he touched her shoulder, and he could see her lean in towards him. When she opened her eyes, it was as if she had just noticed she moved.

"I think you are fine. I think you could make anyone seem attractive because you are naturally hot. I don't want to be on the short end of the stick as we look at the perfect model for why diversity has no downsides."

"Diversity?"

She stepped away from him and crossed her hands

across her chest. "You're hot, and you have parents that are obviously of different backgrounds."

"I guarantee I put on my clothes like everyone else in Sweet Blooms."

"I'm not from Sweet Blooms."

"It's okay. I know there are women who are born outside of Sweet Blooms."

He stepped towards her and placed his hands on her waist. "Trust me. We're friends. I know you may have some concerns, but we'll deal with it together. Don't give up on us before we even start." Vihaan grinned. "I looked up all of the sexy sayings, and I've been dying to say this: "Trust me, I've got this."

She looked him in the eye and then started laughing. "That is the worst saying a guy could ever say."

"You say that, but notice how every time it's said, women still go along. It's a winner."

She looked at him wide-eyed. "I want to say you're wrong, but I can't think of a time when it wasn't true."

"See, you need a fresh mind to look at these things."

She smiled and let out a breath. "Well then, let's do this."

Vihaa's grin widened. "Let's."

She took a seat on the couch and looked at the bolts with obvious skepticism.

"What are we doing today?"

Vihaan picked up the first bolt of cloth. It was a deep blue that called to the black in her hair. He knew next to her skin, it would make her look royal.

"It's my belief that you are trying to do what you do best, which is put definitions and rules to color. Color is a fluid thing. To fix that, I want you to experience color. I've brought four colors that I think will work. Today, I want you to try the cerulean blue. I want you to describe it."

Katherine looked at it and began. "Well, it's—"

Vihaan cut her off. "You can't describe it from afar; it has to be an experience. So stand. I will make a loose sari for you. I've already pre-cut it. I just brought extra in case you fell in love with it."

"You want me to wear it?"

"Yes, Katherine. I want you to see and feel what it's like. I'll help. Stand up."

He could see the look of doubt in her face, but true to her word, she stood, and Vihaan got to work. He pulled the pre-cut cloth off the bolt. He threw the end over her right shoulder so it hung to her waist, and then he loosely wrapped it around her waist and tucked the excess into the faux band he had made.

"You look beautiful," he said as he stepped away from her and opened his arms. He looked at her from head to toe, and it only confirmed his feelings. He wondered if she would be able to see the woman she was now. She was pure and unadulterated in her beauty and her spirit.

"It's time you looked in the mirror." He had to practically pull her along to her bedroom where there was a full-length mirror. Although he didn't understand why, since all of her clothes were practically the same.

When they were in front of the mirror, she looked at herself and then looked at him in the background.

"Okay, what am I looking at? It's a piece of cloth draped across me. I mean, I can't even run in this."

"I can see what you need help with is looking at and appreciating what you see. When you do, this design will come to you as well."

She raised her eyebrow up at him.

"It's true. Trust me."

She nodded. "Well, we've come this far. Let's do this, and then you'll be satisfied that I can't be helped either."

"Close your eyes for now and listen to me. I think the world will open up for you."

After he saw her eyes were closed, he took some of the excess material and dragged it down her arm. He went back and forth as if he were painting. H could feel her tense and then lean into the stroking.

"This feels like silk. It's smooth, cool, and bold all at the same time. The material has no excess pieces hanging out. It doesn't snag the skin. Open your eyes, Katherine."

She did slowly, as if she were getting drowsy from the stroking.

"Look at the blue against your skin. It makes your arms seem like the uniform color palette. The blue has a wave of shine to it that ripples like the blue in your hair. Do you see the blue-black that dances at the ends of your hair?"

She reached up and brought the ends of her hair to the material. "Yes, I do see it."

"This color is like the ends of your hair. The color is there, and it can be bold when we put it on you in the form of a dress or subtle like it is on the ends of your hair. Now I want you to sway from side to side."

He could see her shallow breaths and the way her eyes went back and forth from his reflection in the mirror to the material. Hopefully he had done his job, and she would be able to finish it.

She fastened her eyes on herself and swayed right to left.

"See, you don't need to run. You need to move from side to side. Tell me what you feel."

She placed her hands on her waist and lightly ran her fingertips over it.

"I feel strong. When I move from side to side, I feel like I'm in control."

"When people design things, they pick colors that match, but they also pick colors that speak to them. I want you to hear the colors first before you learn the rules of colors. For the rules, I can give you a book, but for the feel of it, we'll do that together."

By this point, his hands were resting on her waist, moving with her.

"I'm going to kiss you," he said. "You're too beautiful for me to pass up the privilege. Are you okay with that?"

"Yes, I am."

He felt her try to turn, and he shook his head no. Instead, he leaned down and kissed her on the neck. He never broke eye contact with her. He felt her body stiffen, and then he placed another small kiss next to the first.

The taste of her was intoxicating to him. Her skin was smooth. Her scent was fresh, and it was all that and more he thought kissing her would be. He stood up and then dropped his gaze to her hands over his at her waist.

"The request probably kills the spontaneity, but I thought you were too beautiful to resist. I'm still working on being the commercial macho man."

He moved his hands from her hips. When it looked like she was about to say something, they both heard his cell go off.

"Saved by my mom."

She grinned at him. "One of us was."

Ten

Vihaan was stumped. As part of the package of being able to shape Sweet Blooms, he had agreed to take on an apprentice. Adam thought one of the flaws of the town was that there was no training going on. There were a lot of people getting married, but they hadn't had kids yet. No one knew if those kids would stay in Sweet Blooms. Adam believed by offering training from talented people, a new crowd would be attracted to the area. Vihaan was honored and nervous about taking him up on this. He had already known his fair share of people who were shocked to discover he was from Sweet Blooms. There were some who couldn't place him and didn't even consider he might be from the south. Vihaan had expressed his concerns to Adam. Adam brushed them aside and told him to be him. He had told him to let those who wanted to learn find him.

All of that advice had fallen to the wayside this morning as Vihaan looked through the applications of those who wanted to be his apprentice. He was looking at the samples that accompanied the applications. The sample asked the applicant to showcase what they were best at in architecture. He had two left. One of them was a master of color. While the buildings themselves were simple, his use of color and the environment were ingenious. The other sample took bold chances on building design and used green technology to power everything.

Vihaan rubbed the back of his neck as he got up and left his office to go to the communal kitchen. Tea would help clear his head. When he walked into the kitchen, he saw the *you're invited to a wedding* basket from Kelly and Joshua and smiled. It was decorated like a school book bag. All of the boxes looked like school supplies, but when he opened one, he saw there was candy inside.

"Oh, I see I've come just in time," Suhana said. Hearing Suhana brought a smile to his face, and his worries were temporarily pushed away.

"You must have some sort of radar when it comes to chocolate," he teased. He went to the cabinet to get two cups for tea.

"I have a radar for all things that might bring me some pleasure. Chocolate is one, and seeing you, cousin, is the other."

Vihaan remembered what he wanted to say to Suhana.

"I missed you the other day. Is everything alright?"

Suhana smiled. "It's the way it's supposed to be. At least I thought it was until I really looked at your face."

Vihaan grinned. "I didn't think I looked that bad." He thought about the samples in his office and decided to take a chance. "Did I tell you Adam wants me to get an apprentice?"

Suhana took a box out of the basket and began eating. "Nope, but I'm not surprised. Adam sees your potential."

Vihaan bowed. "Thank you, although I think you might be biased. I have narrowed it down to two candidates."

Suhana raised her eyebrows. "Tell me, are they are ravishing beauties and you can't decide?"

Vihaan scoffed. "My heart is taken. The two applicants are so different. The only thing that makes one a little better than the other, maybe, is experience."

"Why does experience matter if you are going to teach them everything?"

"Well, there is teaching and then teaching from scratch. A lot of the designs that will be going up need my attention. If I have someone with a little bit of experience, they can come with me, and I can train while I work. If they have less experience, then I have to move some items around until they get up to speed, and that is assuming they will get up to speed."

"Are you going to meet them?"

He shook his head. "We are doing Skype meetings and phone calls."

"Wow, that bites. If you could meet them face to face, I know you'd know which one to pick. So what can you tell me about them from what you do have?"

"Lucas has more experience. He just graduated and has his license as an architect. He works in housing developments to approve plans. He knows what some of the basics are when it comes to being an architect, but needs to work within the bureaucracy."

"Okay, and the other applicant?"

"Case is younger and has little to no work experience," Vihaan said. He watched Suhana's face scrunch up and rushed in with the other part of his statement. "I like Case better because of his enthusiasm, and because a lot of the samples that he gave to me have been things people experiment with, but I haven't seen it all put together. The downside is, while he wins awards, he doesn't have the experience of working with others, being in a company working with others on a deadline, or even working with state or county regulations. Working with those types of entities can be a game changer for some architects."

"If you weren't worried about the consequences, which is what seems to be holding you back and second guessing yourself, who would you pick?"

"Case," Vihaan said. "The thing is, I have to be worried about the person I pick because this isn't my money or my operation. I need to do what is best for Cade Designs. Lucas has good references that I can check. Case's references are all teachers or coworkers. They're good, but no one is still in a position to really judge what he can and can't do."

Vihaan realized that Adam was trusting him to choose the right person. He wanted to make sure that Adam didn't regret choosing him to head the architect and design group.

Suhana popped another chocolate into her mouth. "Do you have a budget for two or maybe have one for half the time and the other for the latter?"

Vihaan shook his head.

Suhana jumped to her feet. "Well, I guess you'll have to make a decision, and at the very worst you will be wrong, and then you can smile and make it better. By the time they look past that smile, it'll all be better."

"Oh, it's the smile, you say?"

Suhana giggled. "I have to say it works for me."

Vihaan made the tea and placed a teacup in front of each of them. They continued to talk about family and town gossip. When Suhana was ready, and half the chocolate was gone, she got up and kissed Vihaan on the cheek. Then she pulled him into a bear hug.

"You will make the right decision."

Then, just like that, she was gone. Vihaan went back to his office. Then, after looking at the design schedule for Sweet Blooms for the next three years, he picked up Lucas' sample, turned it over, and called him to see when he could come to Sweet Blooms.

Anika knew she had to do something to help Vihaan. She got out of the cab and walked up to Geeta's home.

"This is her home; there's no life to greet me," she muttered to herself. Anika and Geeta had come to Sweet Blooms with hopes of opening up a restaurant that celebrated their culture. When that wasn't going to work, Anika left, but Geeta said she would adapt and make it work. In retrospect, Anika could see this was the beginning of their differences. Anika held fast to their traditions and past.

As she walked up to the walkway, she saw the grass was green and no flowers were out to greet visitors. Anika walked up the stone walkway and thought not even the walkway encouraged a person to walk barefoot on it. Where were the things she knew Geeta had grown up with? Where were the welcoming signs that she was one who lived in conjunction with nature? Then the door opened, and it all became clear what happened to her little sister.

"Ananka," Jerry murmured from the door. It was Jerry, Geeta's husband. Anika liked Jerry. He still couldn't say her name correctly, but she liked him. He was still a good looking man and had a good height. The slight bend in his frame took nothing away from him. Anika just couldn't get past how different he was. He couldn't eat the traditional foods Geeta made. Holidays were a challenge because Geeta had to cook twice as much, as well as vegetarian and non-vegetarian. He was an amazing provider, and Anika would tell anyone who asked that Jerry was one of the most attentive fathers to Vihaan she knew. All of those attributes were great, but in her mind, they didn't excuse the issue that their culture wasn't the same one she and Geeta had grown up with. What would a boy follow if not his father's culture? If the father is good, what boy doesn't want to be his father?

Jerry let Anika in and then stepped out.

"You're leaving?" she asked.

Jerry nodded. "I've got some business to attend to. Geeta is in the backyard setting a table for you."

With that, Jerry excused himself and left. Anika nodded, closed the door, and walked to the back of the house. The house was filled with memories of Vihaan, but none of the pictures or trophies would distract her today. In fact, it was because of Vihaan that she was here today.

After meeting with Suhana and understanding that she wasn't going to help with Vihaan, she had decided to appeal to her sister. She knew Vihaan and Geeta were close, and one of two things would happen today: Anika would understand what her sister was doing, or Geeta would help her to save Vihaan.

Geeta had laid out a blanket, and on it she had laid several brightly colored pillows. In the middle of the blanket was a low table. It was reminiscent of what they would do as children. Anika smiled at the memory. When she stepped out on the back of the house, she placed her sandals next to Geeta's and went to sit on the blanket.

"I made us some tea," Geeta said, motioning Anika to take a seat on the other side. "It has been a long time since both of us sat with each other."

"I thought you had forgotten these times," Anika said, smoothing her hands over the pillows. She saw lemon bars on a small plate and smiled. Geeta had remembered her favorite snack as well. She knew Geeta preferred the small buns to the bars, but she had served the bars.

"I don't forget, Anika, but I'm not a prisoner of those memories either," Geeta said.

Anika looked at Geeta to try and understand the woman she had known so well at one point in her life. Geeta's hair was down, and she was dressed in a long flowing dress that was bright orange with flower petal outlines in a black thread. Anika could see how her bare arms were toned from working in the restaurant. Her arms also bore the marks of a burn or two from being in the kitchen. Geeta hadn't tried to remove them or hide them. She was just herself all of the time. Anika was never sure where Geeta got that courage to just be. It had served them both well to get where they were in the world. But now Anika found herself in the skin of her sister, but with the soul of someone she wasn't sure she knew.

"Stop, Anika. It's not that bad," Geeta said.

"You seem to think so, but I'm not so sure. I thought I knew what I was coming here to do, but when I see you, I'm confused and lost. My baby sister is a wife and a mother, and I'm coming today as a concerned aunt."

Geeta looked at her for a moment. "I wonder, who are you here for today?"

Anika looked away as Geeta poured the tea and served the bars. She thought she would be able to guide the conversation, but as usual, Geeta had a way of getting straight to the core of the situation.

"I'm concerned for Vihaan and for us. I look at Suhana and see she is unhappy. More importantly, she is unhappy and won't have anything to do with me beside duty, just because I give her some advice now and again." Anika brought the teacup up to her lips and let the steam cover her blinking eyes as she thought about how stiff the conversation was between her and Suhana.

"I've been remiss, Anika. I didn't know you felt that way."

Geeta hadn't known? Anika put down her cup and looked at Geeta. "You didn't know? I thought you knew all things. If I said right, it seems as though you would say left. I am alone in the room when the family gathers. I fear that what has happened with Suhana will happen with Vihaan. I will speak what I think is best, and I will be a shadow at our gatherings." Anika put the tea down and took a bite out of the bar.

"Is it so important for you to speak?"

"If you knew that Vihaan was doing something that might hurt himself, wouldn't you tell him?"

"I'd tell him once, Anika. I wouldn't keep repeating it, though."

Anika thought on what Geeta said. "You remember how Suhana was after Zachary passed. There was no comfort for her. She was alone in her grief and used it like a shield. I don't think every mixed marriage ends that way, but what I do think is that it made her feel apart from her family."

Geeta poured herself some tea. "Isn't that the goal? That we hope our children find someone who will stay with them no matter what? Love them no matter what comes, and stand with them through all things?"

"I have stood with Suhana through her wildest periods," Anika snapped back. "I have held her when she dreamed of being a ballerina and they told her no. I have been there when she thought she would be an actress, but she was told she wasn't the right "look." At every opportunity, she has taken whatever I've done and made it seem as though it was a task to be endured."

Geeta leaned back and popped a lemon slice into her mouth. She grimaced for a moment and then gave her attention back to Anika. "What now, Anika? Did you want to tell her she owed you so much for being a mother to her? We choose to be mothers. When a child comes, it doesn't mean you have to mother; you choose. We do it knowing that one day this child will leave and hopefully find more success than us and be happy. We do all of that with the understanding that we may not be a part of that happiness, and still, we do it."

"I wanted so much for Suhana. I wanted to make sure she had the things I didn't. I thought I failed with Suhana, but I wouldn't with Vihaan. I came here to talk about Vihaan."

Geeta nodded slowly and let out a sigh. "I know why

you came. You came to ask me to choose between you and my son."

Anika sat back and looked at Geeta as if she had been struck. "I would never!"

Geeta had a sad smile. "Oh, but I think you would if you thought it was the best thing for Vihaan."

Anika got ready to deny it, but when she played the words over in her mind, she realized Geeta was right. "I don't want him to be alone like Suhana." It was in those moments that Anika realized this whole lunch wasn't going the way she thought it would.

Geeta sat up and poured them both some tea. "I think if you really look at this, you will realize that this isn't about them and the decisions they make, but it's about you and not wanting to be left behind. It can be scary to be alone."

"Children should take care of their elders," Anika said weakly.

"No matter what, you will always be able to get Vihaan or Suhana to give you duty, but I have to tell you that I've seen duty and it is a cold thing to have after you've tasted love."

"I came here thinking I was going to tell you what to do, but you seem to have a better idea of how this works. What should I do?"

Anika looked around and thought about what Geeta said. The backyard had flowers around the perimeter, but when she looked at the deck, she realized it had been built by Jerry and Vihaan. There was a trellis in the corner. It was crooked, and the pattern seemed off. She couldn't say what was wrong, but Anika remembered Suhana and Vihaan building it so they could have tea underneath a trellis.

When Anika thought of her place, she only had pictures of Suhana and Vihaan at Geeta's. Her house didn't have the memories that Geeta's did. Anika wanted family and loyalty, but her home had become a shadow. She didn't want to fade into the background of nothingness. She looked at Geeta and sat up, straightening her spine. Anika knew how to fight. She couldn't think of anything worth fighting for more than family.

"I need your help, baby sister."

Geeta smiled. "I tell everyone if you have the right question, I have the answer. Now let's get to work."

Eleven

"Red is about indulging in your senses," Vihaan said as he guided Katherine to a portable canopy that he'd set up in her backyard. It was draped in beautiful red curtains. Some of them were sheer; some of them were solid.

Katherine had looked at the canopy with suspicion when she first saw it. "Are we reenacting some part of you being the Sheikh and me being a harem girl?"

"I thought I made it clear I'm not looking for anything so shallow. This is all a part of the deep dive into you."

When Vihaan had asked if he could set things up in her backyard, she'd been nervous. She wouldn't confess how many times she had played with the blue material until she got it to look somewhat the way he had it. Katherine had to admit when it was draped across her skin, he was so right. She didn't think the feeling was going to help her be more creative, but she felt more delicate than she ever had.

Today was filled with doubt and anticipation. She knew the next color was red. She expected something that had to do with sex. What else was red for? She had been scouring the internet as well as looking at what else red could do. It made people buy things. It caught a person's attention. All of the information hadn't prepared her for today.

It started with the request of him being able to set up in her backyard. Then came the box. Inside was a red dress with a note that said 'Wear me.' She wasn't some Alice in Wonderland kid who did what she was told, but when she pulled it out and felt the fabric, she decided to give him a pass. It was smooth and cool to her skin.

Then there was the kiss; it wasn't a kiss, but it was. She wanted a kiss. Katherine never knew a kiss could be a tease, but that last kiss was just a primer for the pump. Looking at the dress and thinking about their last kiss, she knew tonight was going to be about being closer. All the signs said so, and all the internet pages confirmed it.

When she got home and dressed and went into the backyard and saw the draped canopy, she was nervous and aroused at the same time. When he stepped out into view, she took him in appreciatively. Tonight, Vihaan had changed as well. He was dressed in loose black pants and a white top that ended at his thighs. The top had a vee that accentuated his chest and made her very aware that he believed in keeping his body as in shape as his brain.

He held out his hand and pulled back the drapes at the same time. It was nothing like what she was expecting. In retrospect, she could say she was expecting something that looked like a bed. Instead, it was a long table with a feast of desserts on it and two chairs. Her doubt and disappointment must have shown because Vihaan leaned down and whispered in her ear, "Trust me,"

She looked at him and shook her head and rolled her eyes. "I do; don't make me regret it!" she said jokingly.

They went to sit at the table, and instantly, the aroma of the food wafted over her as a gentle breeze went through the canopy. Vihaan sat next to her and pulled a small plate out and placed it before her. She looked at the plate and then back at him.

She looked at the spread and then looked at Vihaan and shrugged. "Okay, what am I supposed to do now?" she asked, looking at the table. "This looks like an awful lot of sweets. Did you invite anyone else?"

Vihaan laughed. "No."

"Well, then, I don't get it."

"Red is an amazing color, and it's about the senses. So I thought we'd explore yours."

"With food? I don't know if I'll like—"

Vihaan interrupted her. "The way this works is a little different." Vihaan reached out and picked up a strip of cloth.

Katherine looked at him and then at the black cloth. "So every site I've looked at says red has to do with sex, and then you bring out a blindfold. I'm all for trusting you, but even you have to see how this looks."

Vihaan laughed. "I promise we're not going anywhere, and I wouldn't dare anything at this point in our relationship."

"Why doesn't that make me feel any better?"

"Stop stalling!" Vihaan laughed. She nodded her consent. Vihaan tied it on, and then the world went dark.

"Can you hear me, Katherine?"

"You blindfolded me, you didn't beat me over the head!"

"I'm going to feed you some desserts, and we'll walk through them."

"And is this is going to help me how?"

"It's going to help you to be able to identify and talk about your senses. Red is the color that explores our senses. It gives us the freedom to indulge and be richer for it."

Katherine heard him and nodded.

"Let's start." Katherine was going to ask him when she would know, but then she felt the light brush against her lips. She didn't wait for him to say anything; she waited for the chocolate to go by and took a lick.

"You're starting without me?"

"It's chocolate!"

Vihaan laughed. "How does it taste?"

"Like chocolate."

"How about I go first, and then you taste yours and tell me if you have the same experience."

Katherine was sure this wasn't going to work, but he was determined, so she went along.

"Go for it."

She heard the crunch of Vihaan biting through the chocolate next to her ear.

"This chocolate is fresh. It doesn't have a chalky film on the top of it, and it still smells as if it were a liquid. Sniff."

Katherine inhaled, and the aroma of the chocolate wafted up. "It's milk chocolate," she said.

"You're right. You know when you took a taste of the chocolate a moment ago, it was firm. I'm going to put the chocolate on your bottom lip, and I want you to take a bite."

"I don't do alcohol in chocolate," she said hesitantly.

Instead of replying right away, she felt him blow on her neck right where her neck and shoulder met.

"I don't do alcohol either, so we're in luck. I was curious if you were open for another kiss."

Katherine was already leaning towards that heat. She wanted to rip the blindfold off and tell him she had been waiting for him to kiss her all day. When she nodded, she expected him to say something, but there was no time between her consent and the feel of his lips making their way up her neck to stop at the back of her ear. Then he nibbled on her lobe.

"I want you to take a small bite out of chocolate like I just did of you."

Her breath was coming in small gasps, and the tingling feeling she had that had started in her stomach had traveled into her chest, spreading like wildfire over dry brush. She nodded and gingerly opened her mouth when she felt the weight of the chocolate on her bottom lip. Her mouth opened, and she took a small bite and felt his breath against her neck when he spoke.

"Perfection," he murmured.

She was caught in the midst of a maelstrom of sensation and need. She wanted to melt towards him and let the feeling take her away. Like before, he started her swaying to some rhythm that only the two of them could hear. It shouldn't have been this personal; she knew where they were.

Then she felt him trail a finger along her collar bone, and all thoughts left her.

"Remember this feeling, Katherine. It's about you

owning and experiencing the gifts life has to offer. When you do, you look like a queen."

She opened her eyes and turned to face him.

"A queen that I'm more than willing to follow where she leads."

"Kiss me," she said.

Vihaan shook his head. "Tonight is about sensation and you feeling free enough to experience them."

She couldn't say what had come over her, but she felt drunk on those very sensations he was talking about. "Did you lie? Won't you give your queen this small request?"

Moments later, he angled his head, and his mouth was on hers. He kissed her deeply, making sure not to touch any other part of her. Finally, when she realized he wouldn't move closer, she did.

As soon as her hand found itself in the dark waves of his hair, he broke the kiss and took a deep breath.

"Vihaan," she breathed against his lips. When he opened his mouth, she thought it was to kiss her again; instead, he spoke.

"I've got to go."

Katherine blinked. "What?"

"I've got to leave."

Her feelings went from passion to hurt to anger. "You're going to leave me now? And with all of this untouched food?"

"I underestimated my weakness for you."

"What?"

Vihaan motioned to the tent. "I'll have this removed tomorrow. I thought I could show you to trust your emotions and let go. When you did, I wasn't prepared for your beauty or the sensations you unleash in me."

Katherine took a moment and looked at Vihaan and felt a little better that he wasn't unaffected by their kiss. "I'm a big girl, Vihaan."

He smiled, traced her cheek with his finger, and then leaned down as if he were going to kiss her again. Instead, he hovered over her mouth.

"You may be a big girl, but I'm the man here. I didn't come to seduce you. I came for you to embrace yourself and got caught in the storm. I'm leaving because I respect you. I desire you, and when we are together, I want it to be at the right time and under the right circumstances. You are too precious for an impulsive moment."

"Don't I get a say in this?" she whispered.

He shook his head. "Not this time, my queen. Part of service is respect, and I could do nothing else but leave with my dignity intact."

She sighed in frustration. "Boy Scout! Be careful you don't find yourself back in the friend zone."

He smiled and stood up. "I'll show myself out, but remember how red encompasses bold sensations."

When he left, and she looked at the spread, she shook her head and grabbed some strawberries. "I don't know if I'll survive the next color at this rate."

Katherine should have known she wasn't going to make it out of the office on time. She had a lunch date with Suhana, and she wanted to know what other colors there were. She had discovered she was not a patient person.

"You've got to see what he does with color. I'm sure

he could do something for the board for an advertisement as well," Sandra said.

Hearing Sandra and the click-clack of heels that would herald Clarissa, she knew she had waited too long to leave. The best thing to do was to brazen it out and hope that when they saw she had her bag, it would motivate them to move on.

Sandra gave a wide smile and walked quickly to her. "Are you going out to tell someone they won't be getting any money?"

Katherine stifled her moan of disgust. "It's not my job to make people feel better. It's my job to watch out for Cade Designs' money. If people hear they won't be getting any money, they need to think about the reasons I give."

"Well, then that would be a yes to you going out and being a dream killer," Clarissa said silkily. Sandra murmured in agreement.

"I'm not the bad guy here. I'm trying to help," she protested.

Sandra waved Clarissa off. "Now, don't you mind Clarissa. I'm sure she meant nothing by it. I'm here to see Vihaan. He told me to bring some ideas, and I thought I would bring Clarissa since she's a member of the board and has such great taste in design."

"He's not here, and I'm on my way out," Katherine said, moving towards the door. She hoped they would get the hint and go with her. When they started to move with her, albeit slowly, she thought she was home free. Then they started to talk.

"You've got to see his work. It's hard to concentrate on the work when you see him, but I do my best," Sandra said with a chuckle.

"Oh, is that part of the service of what makes his work so good? Good scenery?" Clarissa asked.

"It's not the only thing, but here in Sweet Blooms, he's exotic looking. I mean, when you look at Jerry, he's a good looking man, and you can see those genes in Vihaan. Although I can only speak for myself when it comes to these matters. I don't know what he did or didn't offer anyone else," Sandra snickered.

Katherine was clenching her teeth as they tittered down the hallway. She had to make sure she chose her words carefully. She didn't like the way they were talking, but she didn't want to burn any bridges with clients of Vihaan's.

"Really, I think that Vihaan's work speaks for itself. Surely whatever natural good looks he may have been born with should have no bearing on his talent," Katherine tossed over her shoulder.

"Let's not shun the power of good looks. Many a person has made a career based on their looks, and their "supposed talent" was accepted as a fad," Clarissa said smoothly.

With that comment, Katherine had to stop and turn around to face the women. "What are you saying?"

Clarissa shrugged her shoulders. "We are all adults here, so let's not act outraged. There has been more than the fair share of pretty faces that may have been able to do the rudimentary concepts of the career they had chosen, but were in no way, shape, or form due or entitled to the fame they may have achieved. Physical beauty is appreciated and encouraged to do all sorts of tasks they don't have the natural skill for."

Katherine looked at Clarissa and couldn't believe the woman who had been touted as the town's beauty queen would dare say such a thing. "What are you saying, that you came out here to share ideas or to test if he really had any talent?"

Clarissa shifted her pose to one hip. "I'm not here to test him. He's young and more than likely talented. He's not someone we can count on to do what's best for the town or our culture. I'm here to represent the board and make sure none of the visions as the board has heard them are too loud when we think about the town culture."

"What is your concern based on? Has he designed something that was so out there or beyond what you are looking for that you need to watch him?" she asked Clarissa. Then she turned to Sandra. "Was there anything in your conferences that made you think this person doesn't understand the atmosphere that you're trying to create?"

"No, not yet…"

Katherine looked between the two women, waiting for an answer.

Sandra sighed. "He's provided several visions—some tame and some pushing the boundaries—but I can't say that any of them would be foreign or disparage the makeup of Sweet Blooms."

Katherine looked at Clarissa. "Do you have proof that he does not understand the culture in Sweet Blooms?"

"You know he was raised a little different than you or me. You know that he is different," Clarissa responded.

"What I know is that he is a person. What I know is I was not born in Sweet Blooms, so you don't know if I was raised a little different. What I know is he has been able to perform every task that we have given him. I'm a little surprised by you of all people, Clarissa. A lot of people would say that a pretty girl can't be smart. But you are sitting on the board of the town proving all of them wrong. We need to give Vihaan a fair chance. And to be honest, I am truly shocked that I would be having this conversation with either of you."

Katherine had worked in many small towns. She was extremely surprised to find that small town mentality against Vihaan in Sweet Blooms. If anything, she expected the town to have a problem with her because she was the stranger.

Sandra had been looking between Katherine and Clarissa; finally, she spoke up. "Katherine, I hear you, but I have to say I think you are turning this into a big deal. Vihaan's work will have to prove itself just like anyone else's. Isn't that what you want?"

Katherine nodded. "It is what I'm looking for, but I don't want Vihaan to have to start form a negative deficit. I go to towns all the time on behalf of Cade Designs. People see me and make all kinds of assumptions. It's true my work speaks for itself, but it's harder on me for no other reason than I'm different, or they stereotype me, and I have to work twice as hard to break it."

Sandra sighed. "You know, Clarissa, I think Katherine might have a point. Vihaan is very talented. He has been the most professional and outgoing person I've ever worked with when it comes to designing the community center. I'm making quick judgments because of the way he looks, and because he had mixed parents. In truth, he's Sweet Blooms too."

Katherine could see Clarissa standing with her arms over her chest and her lips pursed. Clarissa was unhappy. "Since you're so sure, Sandra, you can review his work. But hear me when I say you have the final decision on what will be done. If it turns out to be offensive or too vibrant, then we will intervene."

Katherine shook her head. "I think the design of the building is Sandra's responsibility. If Vihaan can't make her happy, then they need to address it. Let Vihaan and Sandra work it out."

Clarissa waved it off and then plastered on a smile. "You can do whatever you want, Sandra." Clarissa turned to Katherine. "The problem is, I understand way more than you may think I do. I know beauty changes a person." With that, she walked out with Sandra, leaving Katherine to think maybe there was more going on.

Twelve

"I couldn't believe the craziness I was hearing," Katherine said as Suhana passed her the ketchup. "They spoke about him like he wasn't from Sweet Blooms. As if because he had mixed parents, he wasn't worthy enough to be a Sweet Bloomer. I just didn't get it. I've been in that spot when people make up judgments about me based on what I look like. And to see Clarissa participating in that type of behavior was just disgusting. He's been here forever. Why are they treating him like this?"

Suhana reached out and pulled the plate of fries closer to her and pushed the empty plate in front of Katherine.

Katherine looked at the plates on the table and noticed how Suhana was munching away on the side dishes only.

"Is it that you don't eat meat? And can you really consume all of that fried food without getting sick?"

Suhana smiled. "I'm blessed with a very good constitution. I can eat anything and will try everything at least once. I am not against meat. I just prefer fish," she said as she popped another fried zucchini stick into her mouth.

Katherine looked at the plates and lined them up in front of Suhana. Suhana grinned at her and continued to pop the fried appetizers in her mouth.

Katherine grabbed a tater tot off the plate nearest her. "What was I saying before I was so distracted by your ability to consume all things?"

Unfazed, Suhana answered, "Oh, you were going on and on about how women were unfair to Vihaan. Treating him like some piece of meat to be admired instead of seeing his amazing talent as an architect and a designer."

Katherine could hear the faint sarcasm in her voice. "I'm not being obtuse about his looks."

Suhana waved the fry in her hand. "Obtuse. SAT word. Unfortunately, I'm not surprised."

Katherine sighed. "They were accusing him of not understanding the culture and vision of Sweet Blooms. He has provided them with several options that fit what they were looking for, and she still went on to say that maybe he wouldn't be able to understand the finer points of designing for Sweet Blooms."

"Vihaan is very attentive when it comes to things he likes. He can produce designs for all people because that is his passion."

When Suhana said passion, Katherine's mind went back to the tent and strawberries. "I agree; he can be very passionate about things."

"I think we are talking about a little more than just his designs," Suhana said with a smile.

"He's been very respectful and hasn't done anything inappropriate."

"There's a lot of space between respectful and doing something."

Katherine gave Suhana a second look. "I thought you were okay with Vihaan and me helping each other."

Suhana locked gazes with her. "I'm okay with whatever makes the two of you happy," she said in a conspiratorial tone. "I just want you to be aware that being around Vihaan may come with some backlash. He's part of Sweet Blooms, but some people would say only half. You're new to Sweet Blooms altogether."

"I don't think when I spoke up for him that I was out of line. As a professional, I respect Vihaan. I spoke up for him because he wasn't there to speak for himself."

Suhana moved two plates out of the way.

"I agree with what you did. I'm just worried about everyone these days."

"We're friends."

"He's showing you colors and helping you find your inner woman. It's an old custom that came from oral tradition in our family. But we all know how it ends. The man uncovers the woman underneath, and then the woman emerges and decides if she wants the man or not."

Katherine listened, enthralled by the tale. "I didn't know."

"You wouldn't, but Vihaan does. So I'm telling you, you may be friends now, but his intention isn't for that to be a permanent state."

"I think it's a great story and so romantic, but I think I will break this story. I think when the man uncovers the woman, she's a swan after all. She is good, but I have to tell you, as good as a teacher Vihaan is, I don't think he's going to be able to do anything more than putting a bow on this little piggy. A beautiful bow, but that's all it will be—outside fluff."

Suhana gave her a wan smile. "You are trusting Vihaan with something no man has seen. The experience, when it's done, will move you more than you know."

Katherine heard Suhana but didn't let the words sink in. She knew herself. She knew that Vihaan was attractive and all, but at the end of the day, she knew herself.

"I'll be careful and fine, Suhana."

"You are a seed sleeping, Katherine. When Vihaan wakes you up, you may see him differently."

"We'll see." Fortunately, the waitress came and distracted Suhana with more appetizers. Katherine appreciated Suhana's words, but she knew the truth. When it was all said and done, Vihaan would be disappointed that he couldn't find the epitome of women inside her. She was better than when she started, she'd say that, but to be able to embrace her emotions and design like Suhana wasn't even reasonable. She was grateful for what she had and whatever else he could do, but she didn't expect it to go beyond this assignment. She was on Vihaan's list now. When a new assignment came along, he would throw himself into that as well.

Anika knocked on the door to the temporary office. She knew Vihaan was out, so she would have an opportunity to talk to Katherine. She had Geeta's words in her heart, and she was ready to be open-minded when it came to Katherine.

She had rehearsed how she would talk to Katherine.

She held Suhana close to her chest and knew that this reaching out session she was doing was what would be the best for everyone. If she didn't find a way to make peace with Katherine, then she would lose one of the most important things to her. Anika was ready and willing to fight for her family.

She knocked on the door again, but there was no answer. She grabbed the handle and walked in. The air was cooler inside, and she could see right away the person she had come to see and why they hadn't opened the door. Katherine was on the phone, and it looked like whomever she was on the phone with, it was an animated conversation. When Anika walked down the hall towards Katherine, her head popped up, and whoever was on the other line, she was closing the call.

Anika stood in the doorway with a polite small on her face as Katherine seemed a bit flustered.

"I didn't hear you," she said in defense of herself. "When I'm in the office, I can barely hear myself over the air conditioner."

Anika remembered Geeta told her to loosen up. "I thought for a moment you were ignoring me."

Katherine's mouth tightened. Anika couldn't tell if it was in defense or unhappiness. Instead of replying to that comment, she motioned for her to take a seat in the chair in front of her desk.

"Did you want me to call Vihaan?" Katherine asked.

Anika reached out and laid her palm flat. "No, please don't. I came here for you."

With those words, Katherine sat back in her chair and looked at Anika. "I don't know if I should be happy or scared."

Anika looked around the office. "I can see the space must be good for you to work," she said, taking in the windows strategically placed to allow light into the rooms. "I wonder why you haven't updated the walls beyond the factory colors. I know you must be busy, but certainly you'd like to have some more color to keep your spirits up when you work."

Katherine had on her suit, and she straightened her back and looked at Anika.

"These aren't the factory colors; these are the colors I chose to work in. I find them calming," Katherine said. She folded her hands in front of her on the desk.

"Now that we've discovered that my style or preference in color doesn't suit you, can you tell me why you came by today?"

"I came by to see you. We are a close family, and Vihaan spends a lot of his time working and being here. I wanted to see the place where he works and who he works with. As I said before, I came for you."

Anika didn't know how Katherine could be so snippy. She thought about what she had said, and really, she should be happy that she mentioned the drab colors to her. She was doing her a favor. She could see how it may not be taken that way, but shouldn't a woman take advice from her elders?

Katherine sat back in her chair, looking at Anika as if she were some sort of new thing she had never seen.

Anika could see Katherine resisting their customs already. This would be a mountain that Vihaan would face. He would love a woman who would push him away from the family he also loved and who nurtured him. Geeta's words about letting him choose his own way fell to the side as she imagined a future of pain for Vihaan.

Vihaan would love this woman with everything he had. Make this woman the center of his universe, and she may give him some happiness, but she would rob him of his family. A person couldn't have two firsts. The heart would make room for two loves, but the head would prioritize them.

Anika needed to find some middle ground that they could agree on. For everyone's sake, she had to find something.

"I know nothing about you. I know you are here for Cade Designs, which is a big company, and you're a woman, so you must be very good at what you do. I know how hard it can be for a pretty woman to move up in the world and be respected."

Katherine seemed to relax a bit. "Yes, it's been challenging, and I've worked very hard to make sure the faith that Adam put in me isn't misplaced."

"How does your family deal with your success?"

Anika could see talking about family was a sore point. Katherine tensed in the chair and looked Anika in the eye.

"I don't mean to be rude, but I wish you would tell me what it is you would like to know. I know you said you came here to get to know me, but why does it matter?"

"I'm here because Vihaan is passionate about this work. He spends a majority of his time working so he doesn't get to go out as much as I would like him to."

"Yes," Katherine said, motioning her to move along.

"Passions can be misconstrued when they are together. You two work together a lot, and he may think his passion could lie with you. I wanted to know if you were interested in having a relationship with Vihaan or if this was just a working relationship."

Katherine was stock still for a moment, and then a small smile came upon her.

"Why don't we go into the kitchen. I think I need something to drink, and there is an appetizer tray in there from an earlier meeting. We can talk there."

Anika was confused by her change in attitude, but she'd follow this through to find out what her intentions were. "That would be nice," Anika said.

She followed Katherine into the kitchen and saw the plate of crackers, jam, and dip. Anika looked around and saw how Katherine pulled out the drinks and glasses as well. After taking a bite of the cheese, she was pleasantly surprised by the taste.

"Did you make the plate? It's well put together, and the tastes go well with the crackers and cheese," Anika asked.

"No, I ordered it."

"Oh, you didn't have time this time. When you make your own, what do you use?"

Katherine sat down at the table and looked across at Anika before she spoke deliberately and popped a cube of cheese in her mouth.

"I don't make plates. I pay for them. I don't organize teas or put pretty colors together either. In fact, when it comes to the things that I think you are referring to, I think I'm pretty inept. However, I do know how to call a caterer. I'm a master when it comes to budgeting, and I can find the talent it takes to make any project pop."

Anika tried not to clench her teeth during the litany, but she was hearing all of her worst fears. "This isn't what I would have expected for someone who would be with Vihaan."

Katherine nodded. "I'm glad we are both clear on what is not happening here and why."

When Anika saw Katherine standing up, she realized that her questions hadn't been interpreted as helpful but that she was critical. "I'm not here to criticize if that is what it seemed like. I'm just watching out for Vihaan like family does for one another."

"I'm sure you are doing what you think is best."

Seeing Katherine's face set in stone, Anika decided it was best to leave. "I'm sure you have other things to do, and I don't want to take up any more of your time."

As Anika stood up to leave, she thought she saw Katherine blinking as if she were holding back tears. Anika shook her head. No, Katherine had made it clear she was happy with the way her life was. She must have imagined the blinking.

Thirteen

"You haven't given me the time of day today."

Katherine looked up to see Vihaan at her office door with puppy dog eyes. She wanted to relent, but then she thought about Anika yesterday, and she held her tongue.

"Ah, now, whatever that thought was, we need to examine it because it is obviously the root of the problem," Vihaan said, advancing into her office.

"I think you should leave it alone."

Vihaan kneeled beside her desk and looked up at her from bended knee. "How could I leave my queen? Come on, tell me what is it. I'll fix it. Give me a chance," he said with a smile.

She looked at him at her feet with his earnest look. A hint of devilish laughter lurked behind his eyes. She fought the smile that came to her lips.

"You can't fix your family and how they love you," she murmured.

Putting his hand on her forehead, he sounded distressed when he looked back at her.

"Tell me, was it the rambunctious Suhana?"

Katherine shook her head.

"Ah, someone who thought they were being helpful and wise. I know it wasn't my mom, so that only leaves one woman. My well-meaning Anika?"

Katherine shrugged.

"Did she give you some good woman test that was one step from asking you if you had a chain that was attached to the stove?"

Katherine laughed. "It felt that way."

"I see I need to do much more groveling to make this up to you. How about we pick up some really bad takeout food and go to your place. I'll drive you home and pick you up in the morning to make up for this offense."

Katherine laughed and nodded her head. Then Vihaan stood and held out his hand.

"Then, come, your carriage awaits, and I'm here to serve."

She smiled. "You're getting this male chivalry thing down to a science."

When she stood, they were face to face. Katherine could see his chest rise and fall, but they weren't touching. Then he spoke. "So, you're not looking at me and seeing someone who could only be in the friend zone?"

Katherine swallowed and then looked up into his eyes. "You've got potential to make it out. Now stop stalling and let's get food."

Vihaan looked as though he would say something else, but at the last minute, a smile came over his face, and he stepped back and bowed, motioning her to go past. "Your carriage awaits."

The ride to the Korean takeout place was quiet. When they finally made it to her house and were sitting at the table with all of the boxes opened, she spoke.

"I have to say, I was very challenged with your aunt today," Katherine started as she served the steamed vegetables to herself and Vihaan. "She came in and said it was about me, but it was very clear that she wanted to protect your virtue from me."

Vihaan almost choked when she made that comment. He had to stand up, hit his chest, and then he could laugh out loud.

"You should have told her I was still in the friend zone, and she would have left you earlier," he teased.

"Nothing short of I'm leaving town or already married would have made her leave me alone. She couldn't find a thing about me that was good enough for you."

"Then it's her shortcoming that she can't see how great you are."

Katherine smiled. "Oh yeah, you're getting good at giving out the lines as well."

"I'm doing my best, but I have to say it's all due to my inspirational teacher."

"Really, all joking aside, I don't want to cause you any trouble with your family."

"I know."

Katherine looked at him as he dug into his food. "Is that it?"

Vihaan looked up at her and then looked at the table. "I'll eat some more."

"Vihaan, I'm not talking about the food. I'm talking about your family."

He reached for another carton and poured some gravy on his vegetables. "I can see this run-in with my aunt has put you off a bit. I want you to know I'll take care of it. She's overreacting because of family history, but still, you shouldn't have to deal with it. I'll talk to her."

She was so grateful that he didn't blame her in any way. "I still feel bad for her, Vihaan. I think she had only the best intentions for you when she came to see me."

Vihaan put the carton down and pushed his plate away. He reached out and gathered her hands in his.

"I will talk to Anika. It's true; she may have the best intentions, but at the end of the day, I'll make my own choices. Now let's change the subject so our night doesn't end on a sour note."

Katherine laughed and agreed. "How are the designs going at the community center?"

"It's moving. Every time I think we have settled on a theme, she sees something else and decides that is the best thing ever."

Katherine laughed as she imagined Sandra Waters saying that. She looked at him and saw he was a little lackluster in his description of the issue.

"Is that all? It seems odd you would be so down or not as upbeat with Sandra because she thinks all of your designs are great."

"I'm mulling over a decision I've made."

"You? That doesn't seem right. I know you are usually very confident with the color choices and combinations you decide on."

Vihaan smiled. "I'm glad you noticed."

Katherine waved him off. "Stop stalling. What's the problem?"

"You're right. I'm fine when it comes to design and combinations, but I had to make a decision about a person, and I'm not as settled on my choice as I would like to be."

"Did you get a feeling that something wasn't right?"

"It's funny to me that now you would be talking about feelings. I didn't use my feelings to pick an intern. I used the facts."

"Okay, then what's the problem?"

He looked up at her and smiled. "My feelings weren't happy with it."

Katherine rolled her eyes. "I always go with my feelings, especially when it comes to people."

Vihaan shrugged. "It's done, and it's too late now."

Katherine stood up and cleared the table. When she was done, and Vihaan had placed all the dishes in the sink, she could see it was still on his mind. She tapped him on his shoulder.

"It's never too late, and if you feel it is, remember you can always change your mind. That prerogative isn't just for women."

He was about to answer when his phone rang. Katherine smiled at him and pointed toward his cellphone. "You see, this is a prime example. It's your prerogative again to answer the phone."

Vihaan didn't get to answer because the phone rang again, and then he picked it up.

"Hello?"

Katherine looked at Vihaan's expression go from playful to concerned to aggravated. Then she heard him respond.

"Are you sure?"

He blew out a breath. "I'll be there in a few."

Vihaan lifted his phone and then looked at the kitchen. "I'm sorry, Katherine. I'll make this up to you. I have a problem with an incoming shipment."

"No, no, go and take care of it. I'll be fine."

"Thanks for being so understanding."

Vihaan left, and Katherine got to cleaning up the rest of the kitchen. While she was cleaning, she would occasionally check her phone, making sure she hadn't missed a call or text from Vihaan in case he needed her.

Katherine awoke the next morning to someone ringing her doorbell. She had already gotten up and done her morning yoga, but it wasn't a work day, so she wasn't expecting anyone. When she got to the door, Vihaan was standing outside with a box from the Sweet Blooms café.

Katherine didn't have a lot of weaknesses, but the Sweet Blooms café was definitely one of them. She opened her door to see him leaning against the frame.

"It must be bad if you came with desserts," she said. Then he lifted up his other hand, and it had a carton of coffee in it.

"Good morning," he said.

"Is it?"

"You opened the door. It just got better."

She took the carton from his hand and led him into the kitchen.

"What happened?"

"The orders were doubled, and some of the colors were changed by Sandra Waters. She said she had the authority to do so because it was her project. Since it's a local vendor, they didn't think to check. I can use some of it, but a lot of it is a waste and customized."

She'd already started receiving calls from vendors asking if she wanted to extend the credit for the project, and if she wanted to add Ms. Waters' name as well. Katherine told them she'd get back to them, but she wanted to hear what Vihaan said first.

"I'm thinking of making a kids room, that way I can think about using the colors that are here. Lucas and I are looking at how we can use the materials in a constructive way. The time to get all the materials here is coming to an end quickly."

Vihaan was excited when he said the words, but Katherine could hear the slight hesitation in his voice when he spoke about the construction material. She opened up the Sweet Blooms box and passed him a pastry. He pushed the pastry to the side and placed his hand over hers. It was intimate and reassuring to Katherine. This man who seemed to have it all together, who had all of this talent, wasn't so full of himself that he didn't know how to reach out for comfort from another person, much less her. Vihaan had already given her so much; she couldn't help but place her hand over his.

"You've got this," she said, gazing into his eyes. "I have to admit, accounting me was like, OH NO! Look at that money just rolling out the door. But the woman me who has been getting in touch with herself said this is a time for us to sink into our blueness and calm down. You will see a way out of this, and it will appear like you meant it all along."

"Thank you. Adam gave me a call and said he understood, and if we needed him to, he could move some things around if I needed more time." He gave her a wan smile. "I was happy for the offer, but I've never missed a date for a project, and I don't want to start now."

"Good, because I would hate for it to happen on my watch." She pulled her hands back and picked up her coffee. "You'll be able to use all of the material she ordered. Just think on it, and whatever you come up with, she can't say anything because she was the one who actually purchased it."

Vihaan smiled. "I thought about saying that, but it's not my way."

"I know. That's how I know you'll have this fixed in no time."

"This happens, and at the same time, it forces me to use Lucas and see if he can use some creativity to use the excess supplies."

"How did Lucas handle the latest issue?"

"He was fine. He called me, and then he called the other vendors to prepare them for a delay if need be. He's gotten all of the codes extended and the permits extended as well."

"It seems like all is going well. What's the problem?"

"We have all of this excess material, and he hasn't given me a spec on how to use it yet."

Katherine understood what it was like to make decisions and then have to stand by and see if they panned out or not. It could be nerve-wracking. A person could think they understood the dynamics, but it would have to be played out in front of everyone.

"Listen, Adam and I did our research. You are the right person for this project and for the town. I know you struggled with the decision, but either way, we are behind you. Wait for things to mess up, don't invite them."

"My mother told me great advice comes from women."

"Well, if I have that kind of endorsement, we shouldn't even be having this conversation."

He leaned in and rested his forehead against hers. Then he reached up with his hand and caressed her cheek. After the first pass, they both pulled back, laughing.

Katherine wiped the powdered sugar from her cheek.

"I forgot I touched the donut," he said.

"No, it's okay. I guess I should be honored that I made you forget a Sweet Blooms pastry." After she had put down the napkin, she tapped the table to get his attention.

"Hey, remember what's most important is that we're friends. We're here for each other. So whatever problems we may have, we can bounce them off of each other with no repercussions."

"Does this push me back into the friend zone?"

"No, it puts you into the trusted zone. I think men have a fear of being open. I think women like to know they aren't the only ones with insecurities. Trust is a bedrock of any relationship."

She watched his face as he listened to her. She let her gaze take in every facet of how he looked at her. Then he leaned over and placed a light kiss on her lips.

"Katherine, you are a gift beyond compare," he breathed. The moment was so intense, and she was on the verge of saying things that were so alien to her; she sat back and made light of the situation.

"The sugar has gone to your head. Thank you for the treat, but I think you have a miracle to weave."

"Thank you," he said.

"Anytime you feel like bringing some pastries, I'll be more than happy to help you talk things out."

Fourteen

Vihaan decided to make a party out of the extra supplies. He placed them all outside on the lawn in front of the pond. Then he catered lunch and put up white boards all around so people could draw their ideas, as well as comment on some drafts he had around already. The staff was thrilled to have a working lunch outside on the lawn, and Vihaan said it was a great team booster.

When he went looking for Katherine, her found her sitting on a bench a little ways away from the crowd and closer to the pond. She saw him coming, and it was all becoming so clear that color lesson or not, Vihaan had definitely introduced her to her feelings.

Vihaan had on his blue jeans that always seemed new and a vee neck shirt that was orange. She didn't know how he did it, but he could wear any color and look refreshing. If she wore that color, she could imagine herself looking like a walking orange. If she got sunburned while wearing it, she'd be a walking lobster.

"I can tell from the way you were staring at me that you like this shirt and wish you had bought it first," he said as he took a seat on the bench next to her.

"Oh, I was thinking about something."

"I can see you've decided to provide lunch for me. What else could it mean that you are sitting here with this feast in front of you?"

Katherine laughed. She put a paper plate in front of him and then put a box in front of him.

"I'm not so sure about it being a feast, but I will say it was very considerate of you to provide box lunches for everyone. I only picked up this box because it suspiciously had your name on it," she said to him. "How did you know I would be at that table to get the box?"

Vihaan smiled. "I'll confess, I had no idea which table you would go to. I did know you would go last, so I put my name on about twenty boxes, hoping you'd find one."

Katherine covered her mouth to stop the laugh that bubbled up. "I am truly impressed with your planning."

"I told you. You are the woman I'm trying most to impress."

"You are saying that because you are teaching me about color, which, by the way, I am very appreciative of, and it is working in subtle ways, in case you hadn't noticed."

Katherine fingered the color of her pastel pink shirt.

Vihaan nodded appreciatively.

"Like I was saying, I am not the kind of woman you really like. You like those women who leave tracks on the ground."

"Tracks on the ground?" he repeated, confused.

Katherine lifted her hands and waved them in the air like a Hawaiian dancer. "You know, the women who are so light and delicate they barely ever touch the ground, and when they do they leave only the barest impressions on the earth."

"If she's so light, she can't like eating. I don't think I like these track women."

"Ah, you say that now, but when one walks by you, your head will turn and you'll say, 'how does she do that?'"

"I hope this isn't your answer to why I shouldn't like you."

"No, I'm amazing, and of course you should like me, but I may not be the one for you."

"Well, let it not be said you didn't know you were a prize. I assure you I have had a long time with me, so I feel qualified to pick the one for me."

A staff member came by before she could respond. They were thrilled with the contest and thanked Vihaan for keeping the work environment so open. A couple of others came by, and then Vihaan turned his back to the crowd, and it was as if it were a secret signal to them all not to approach. Then he focused on her. He told her about some of the wild ideas that Suhana had given him for the extra material. He made her think of an idea, and they teased each other by making a more outrageous idea than the last one.

This wasn't the friend zone. He was close enough that their knees touched. He made jokes that made her laugh. He was so smart that their conversation could jump from politics to religion to cooking. He was everything the fairytales said he would be. The thing that attracted her the most was his humbleness.

It occurred to her in passing that no one was making a deal about them sitting at a table alone at a company function. The sun was out, and there was just enough breeze from the pond to keep the insects away. They had finished their food and were laughing about a joke when she heard her name.

"Hello, Katherine."

Katherine could feel the sun getting a little dimmer. The sounds of the surrounding staff seemed to lower, and even the breeze from the pond died down. All that was missing was some storm clouds in the sky.

She looked over Vihaan's shoulder to see Anika standing on the other side of the table. Instead of being dressed in one of her long flowing dresses, she was in a pair of jeans with a blue blouse.

"Hello."

Vihaan turned his body to face Anika. Then he reached out and took Katherine's hand in his. Anika's gaze fell onto their hands. Her jaw was clenched when she addressed Katherine.

"Does he mean nothing to you?"

"Aunt Anika, I'm no child. I choose her willingly."

Anika looked at Katherine. "So you two are out in the open. In front of the coworkers as well. I wonder what they think?"

Katherine sighed. "They don't think anything. We are having lunch, nothing more."

"Is that what you think is being seen? I see the woman who controls the money for a project and a man at her side." Anika turned to Vihaan. "What about your reputation? How will this appear?"

"How does it appear?"

"I already told you," Anika said.

"You think it looks like the talentless boy is trying all he can to keep favor with Katherine. I'm not sure who should be more offended, me or Katherine."

Anika shook her head at his question. "You can't afford to be naïve, Vihaan."

Katherine listened to both of them and said nothing. This was the kind of interplay she had never had. Her family didn't have these conversations. Anika was wrong, but still, she seemed like she was trying to help Vihaan.

"Now you can tell me what I can and can't afford? When am I my own man?"

Anika folded her arms over her chest. "I am here for you. To make sure you are being looked after."

"I'm my own man."

"Then tell me, Vihaan. Who is this woman? If you are your own man, then it's time to do the right thing. You say you make your own decisions. You stay around her all the time. You spend money on showing her the colors as if you were courting, but you haven't brought her around your family. Who is she?"

Katherine was torn. She wanted to stand up and say she was no one that Anika needed to meet, but she wasn't sure. She remembered the blue and red. She thought about how they shared pastries and talked out problems. Was it all a part of their deal? Vihaan was so nice. He said he wanted to be with her, but in light of all Anika said, maybe she needed to have the wake-up call. She needed to understand what was really going on between them. Just as she was going to answer, Vihaan spoke.

"She is the woman who I hope will be my best friend and companion," Vihaan said.

Anika stopped. "What?"

"You always taught me it is a woman's choice to accept a man. How could I tell you something I don't know?

I hoped I could show her what it would mean to be with me, but I have to say that you've given her every reason to turn from me. I know you mean well, Anika, but this is not a family affair. If she chooses me, it will be our decision."

Anika looked at Katherine and then at Vihaan and smirked. It wasn't loud. In fact, Katherine didn't think there was anyone who was at the lunch who heard the exchange. When Anika smirked and waved off Vihaan's comments, Katherine braced herself. She had been on the vicious end of one too many women not to know when something bad was coming.

Vihaan cocked his head to the side. "Why the smirk, Anika?"

"I am foolish. This is a phase. You are right. I will leave you alone, and this project will pass, and so will this. There is nothing she has that you need or our family needs. I was too eager."

Katherine waited for the hole to open up. She looked down at her lap and tried to blink back the heat of tears that lurked behind her eyelids. There was no answer. This was Vihaan's family, and she knew she wasn't even in his life. The only answer was to brush it off. She would wait until Anika left and then excuse herself for the day.

"I know you can't understand because you don't know Katherine," Vihaan said. He looked at Katherine and reached out and caressed her cheek, then turned back to Anika.

"Katherine has all of the attributes you told me to look for in a woman. She's strong. Strong enough to listen to me. Strong enough to tell me I'm wrong. She's brave enough to try new things. The thing I admire the most about her is that she's true to herself. She doesn't change for the whims of others. She stands for what she believes in. She's the woman that fairytales are made of. She's the woman any man would be fortunate to have, and hopefully she'll look favorably upon me."

Katherine knew the words were for Anika. She knew that this was to save face for her because Vihaan was that kind of man. To everyone else listening, they would probably believe them, but Katherine knew the truth. This was all a sham. The words were bittersweet. She didn't realize until he said them that these were the words she had been waiting to hear all of her life. Now that she was hearing them, they were only part of a man doing his best to save her honor instead of garnering her heart.

Anika's hands dropped to her side, and she looked at Vihaan for a moment longer before she sighed. "If this is your vision, then I stand corrected. I will leave you to your quest." She walked as if she still had on those flowing robes. When she was out of earshot, Katherine faced Vihaan.

"I appreciate what you did," she said as she reached out to clear off the table.

"It was nothing. What else could I say?"

Katherine heard his words and echoed them back to herself as well. What else could this good man do but defend her in front of his aunt?

"Don't hold this against your aunt. It seems like she meant well."

Vihaan sighed. "My aunt is lonely and wants to see her former glory lived in someone else's life. If it were my path, then I'd have no problem, but I don't think I'm going down that path."

"Loneliness and lost dreams can make a person desperate," Katherine said.

Vihaan stopped her from cleaning and stood up, bringing her up with him. When she tried to step away, he followed.

"Did you want to dance here?" he asked.

Her gaze looked over his shoulder at other people who were starting to look.

"Let them look. I may not have liked the conditions it happened under, but you are all of those things. You are an amazing woman. You should value you the way you are. Remember, I'm not teaching you anything, I'm just uncovering my woman hidden inside."

She nodded and smiled at him, but inside she was breaking. His woman? No, that was just an expression. He had said it all. What he said to his aunt was nothing. What else could he have said?

Katherine had listened as well, and she knew what had to be done. She had to make sure Vihaan and his family were okay, then she had to make sure they never saw each other again. She wouldn't use his good nature against him.

Two days later, Katherine had a plan, and she was going to make sure it went into effect. She made an appointment to see Suhana to get help. She met Suhana for lattes in town at the coffee shop.

"Hello, Suhana," she said, welcoming her in a wide embrace. Katherine held on a moment longer than she normally would have.

"What's wrong?"

Suhana was once again in one of her beautiful dresses. This time it was a combination of blue and white. With a pair of long blue earrings, she was a gypsy come to life. Katherine realized she was in her business regular today. The same black suit and white shirt.

Suhana gave their order and then looked at Katherine.

"Okay, what did he do now? It hasn't even been that long."

"He didn't do anything."

"Then why do you look like you are about to go to a funeral?"

"Let me explain." Katherine explained Anika coming to the lunch and what was said. By the time Katherine was done, Suhana had gone through every emotion imaginable.

When the story was done, Suhana sat back, wide-eyed.

"Well, I know my aunt can be determined, but I never knew she was this determined. As for Vihaan, he's just slow. You must know he didn't really think it was nothing. He didn't step in because of duty."

Katherine couldn't even remember the day without having to take a minute and not tear up.

"Suhana, when we first started, you know I asked you if you could be my friend."

"Yes?" Suhana replied slowly.

"Well, the time has come."

"Katherine, I think you and Vihaan need to talk."

"We did, and every time he does, he weaves his words, and I fall into some la la land of what I think I want to hear. It's not his fault, and I'm not saying he's doing anything wrong. I'm saying that I'm here to do a job.

Your aunt Anika is right. I will pass. I need to break up with him or in the very least let him know we are just co-workers."

"And how will you do that?"

"I'm not sure yet, but what I want you to do is to go reassure your aunt. Tell her that you spoke to me and I told you I won't be seeing Vihaan. I don't think it's fair for a woman who loves him so much to suffer."

"Katherine, I still think—"

Katherine held up her hand. "Suhana, are you my friend or not?"

Suhana gritted her teeth. "I am."

"Then do this for me."

Suhana stared at Katherine for a minute. So much so, Katherine was scared she was going to say no.

Finally, Suhana nodded. "I will deliver your message loud and clear to Anika."

Katherine sighed. "Thank you. I know this puts you in an uncomfortable position, but thank you so much."

Fifteen

The next day, Suhana met Anika in town at the diner. Suhana knew the moment Anika had seen her. Her lips pursed, and she grabbed her bag a little closer to her body. When she came to the table, she sat down and glared at Suhana. When the waitress came by, Anika passed on a beverage.

"You've been busy, so I hear, auntie," Suhana said sweetly.

"I said what had to be said, in case it wasn't clear what each one brought to the table. It had to be made clear."

Suhana kept her cool and didn't shout or argue. She knew that if she lost her cool, this meeting would amount to what so many other meetings had amounted to: an impasse where everyone agrees to disagree without any understanding on either part.

"You felt the need to humiliate her? To make her believe that she could never be enough for him or our family?"

"She's not like us, and she's not what he needs."

The words were like Anika—straight to the point. What made the conversation such a challenge was that

Anika believed she was defending Vihaan. Love could make people do all sorts of things. "When did love have requirements of beauty, culture, or habits?"

Anika sniffed. "They will both get hurt."

"Because they might fall in love and what?" Suhana asked.

"They would fall in love. Vihaan will try to make something work that will isolate him, and she will try to be something she isn't and start to dislike herself as well."

Suhana could see how she had come to the conclusion. In fact, if Suhana thought on it, she could probably think of a person or two who had the same experience. "We have to trust they can find their own way."

"I'm his aunt, and I don't want him to suffer. Am I a villain for that?"

"Helping him and her is one thing; saying she's not good enough or he's just with her for his career is cruel."

"Suhana, look at her. Vihaan is courting a woman who doesn't know she's being courted. He's giving a gift she can't recognize. You think I'm being mean or rude, but if they can't communicate here at the beginning, the gap will get larger as time goes on. If I point out the issues now, do you think they won't notice these same issues later?

It will only get worse. He will want to show her his world. She will feel out of place. She will have to figure out if she's enough, and Vihaan will wait and do all he can to help her, both of them not understanding that they are missing common ground.

How can they survive if they don't have common ground?"

Suhana was saved from answering the question right away when her tea was brought in the to-go cup. She took a sip and thought about what Anika said. She understood what Anika was saying. In fact, Anika spoke in clean, clear, logical facts. It was one of her strengths and one of her weaknesses.

"I know everything you say is a fact. I know you take every point into consideration. You take everything in except for the fact that love changes the rules of the game."

"Love has its limits!"

Suhana nodded sadly. "For some it does, but not for Katherine and Vihaan. We are meeting today because Katherine wanted me to reassure you that she would make sure that any possibility of a relationship was destroyed between her and Vihaan. She loves him enough to walk away, and she doesn't want to get in between him and his family."

Anika leaned forward. "She's doing the right thing?"

Suhana sighed. "She's doing what you think is right, yes. I don't think Vihaan will agree. When he's alone, and she's gone, I want you to remember what you told me. Love has its limits."

With that, she stood up and left Anika behind. The only thing she could think of was the foolish things people did for love. She wondered how any of them would survive.

Vihaan hadn't sat down with Katherine in three days. Every time he wanted to go over or reassure her that Anika's words meant nothing, work interfered.

Today he decided to do all of his work in the office so he would find time before she left the office today. Just as he was finishing up paperwork, Katherine appeared in the doorway.

"Do you have a moment?" she asked.

"Of course." Something was wrong. Today she was dressed in her standard suit. No hint of color adorned her hair or shirt. When she entered his office, she didn't even take a seat.

"This won't take long. I wanted to say thank you for helping me out. I couldn't have had a better teacher when it came to design and color," she said, practically stumbling over the words.

He got ready to stand up, but she held up her hand.

"No, don't bother getting up. It's not necessary."

He could feel the panic starting to set in. He didn't see a way out of this. It was a trap where the walls were closing in, and he didn't know how to make it better.

"You know it's my pleasure to help you."

Her lips curved, but the sparkle wasn't in her eyes. He had seen this smile when she was dealing with customers.

"I think that I should stop imposing on you and we should get back to what's important—business. I think from now on we should focus our attention on the business. That's what brought us together, and we don't want to lose sight of it or disappoint Adam."

It was a good thing he was already sitting; otherwise, he would have fallen into his chair. "This decision to focus on business came from…"

"It's not a new focus, really. Both of us are very ambitious and career focused. Doing anything else just seems wasteful."

"I never objected."

How could things be falling so quickly? Showing Katherine the other side of herself had been his path to showing her how much he cared. He thought for sure when she was comfortable with herself, she would have been able to see them together, and now it was slipping through his hands.

"At any rate, I wanted to say thank you for what you've done, and I'll bring in the cloth tomorrow," she continued.

That was it. He could have let it all go and let her leave if she hadn't asked to return the cloth. "It was a gift. It never has to be returned because it's yours," he said through clenched teeth. "Is this from Anika?"

She folded her hands in front of her chest and clenched her jaw. "I can make my own decisions. I don't need to have a reason to do something."

Vihaan shook his head. "I thought we trusted each other. I thought we were friends." Vihaan saw her hesitate for a moment and then stand her ground. "I thought what we had was stronger than Anika's words."

Katherine blinked and then gave him a sad smile. "Things change, and some things just become clear as time goes on. I would hope we could work professionally together. If that's not going to be possible, let me know, and I'll get someone else to finish up the project here at Sweet Blooms."

"You'd leave?" he asked.

"I'd do whatever I thought was the best thing to do." With that, she turned and left his office. She didn't stop at her office but went straight to the door. Vihaan heard the door close and sat back in his chair, trying to absorb the pain that had been dealt to him.

The next day Katherine didn't even bother trying to go to work. She had spent all of last night dreaming of rainbows that billowed out into bolts of cloths. Behind every color was Vihaan smiling with his arms open. Every time she tried to get close, the cloths would billow around him, and then he would disappear.

Finally, she woke up and hoped some warm tea would help her situation out. Instead, it just made her more aware of what was wrong. She was trying to put it from her mind. She'd had several conversations with herself as she went over all of the facts that Anika had said about why they shouldn't be together.

When she had come home yesterday, she had fallen into a shallow pit of despair and unhappiness that threatened her concentration and sanity all night long. Every time she thought she was over the moment, it came back like a flash flood over what she had lost without Vihaan.

Then the transition came when she was all cried out. It was anger. Anger that she had allowed herself to be brought low by this situation. She rallied herself, asking herself when did one person's opinion become so important?

She had been through too much to let this event bring her down. It was then when she had said those words to herself in the mirror at two in the morning that it came to her. This wasn't an event. This was love. This wasn't someone deciding she wasn't good enough so she would prove them wrong and go and get another job. Somehow she hadn't made the cut to be loved and accepted.

When she woke the next morning, she wasn't feeling strong enough to be with Vihaan in the trailer. She called in and let him know she would be available via email and phone. At first, she thought it sounded like he was running, but then she brushed the thought away. It didn't matter what he thought anymore; she knew the truth.

Now, as the new day was coming up, Katherine had moved into another part of the process: loneliness. She missed him. It was amazing how you could miss a person so quickly. One day they were in your life every day, and the next the space they occupied was empty.

It was the little things, like how she would meet Vihaan in the morning and he'd have pastries. It was the way he would call her as if he were a vendor with an outrageous bill and say things like, "We can settle the bill if you'd have lunch with me."

It was the way he noticed things about her and gave her compliments. If she wore a shirt that wasn't white, he would try to guess her mood. If her hair was up or tied differently, he would say how he liked it. Oh yes, there was a hole in her heart, and she was missing him.

Vihaan was the package of dreams. He looked attractive, he had a sense of humor, and he was attentive. He was also not an option for her. While Katherine didn't believe everything that Anika said, what was clear was that if she were with Vihaan, it would cause a commotion with his family. She knew how precious family could be, and she wouldn't interfere in it.

Hopefully, the pain would fade, and life would go on. She'd remember the feeling just in case that was all she'd ever have in her life—the memory of love.

<h1 style="text-align:center">Sixteen</h1>

"Stubborn, pig-headed, gifted people," Suhana murmured to herself as she went to see Vihaan. Over the last week, she had visited Vihaan and Katherine. Neither one of them were happy. When Anika tried to cheer up Vihaan, he just waved her off and said to her she could do what she liked. He didn't feel like celebrating. It was then that Anika came to Suhana and confessed that maybe she should reconsider. When Suhana heard her mulling over a decision, she decided to help them both. She couldn't stand seeing the both of them so depressed.

She went to see him at work because she had already spoken to Katherine and found out she was working from home. The trailer was so quiet that Vihaan could be heard typing in the back. When she saw him, he looked up expectedly. When he saw her, his face fell, and he went back to his work.

"Wow, you really know how to make a person feel welcome."

"Hello, Suhana. I have work I have to get done." She walked around the desk and then pulled the chair that was in front of his desk to the side. Vihaan stopped typing to watch what she was doing.

"Yes, yes, there seems to be a lot of work going on these days," she said sweetly.

"What are you doing here, Suhana?"

"Trying to stop the madness before it goes too far."

"She doesn't want me. She thinks I'm different too. She thinks—"

Suhana held up her hand. "Before you go on the long wail, what I think the issue is is a communication one."

"I talk to her all the time!"

"The issue isn't your talking; it's what you say."

Vihaan looked appalled. "You know me! I've never spoken ill—"

"Not ill, just carelessly. Perhaps when our aunt paid you a visit, you might have said things like it was nothing or what else could you do?"

She watched Vihaan get ready to defend himself again, and then she saw the moment when the memory came back to him and the sinking realization of what it had all meant to her. Shaking his head, he looked at Suhana.

"No, she couldn't have thought that?"

Suhana looked at him and blinked and nodded her head. Vihaan let his head fall into his hands as he murmured to himself about his callous words.

"Why didn't she say something?"

Suhana sat back and looked at him. "Say what, Vihaan? Was she supposed to ask you if you really said nice things to auntie because honor demanded you defend her? I think there are some questions we are too afraid to ask. Especially if we think we know what the answer will be."

Vihaan turned to Suhana and smiled.

"Ah, but you've been talking to her. You could tell me what she thinks so I can fix it."

Suhana held up her hand. "You want me to betray a friend? To tell you something she may have told me in confidence?"

"Suhana, please?"

"Well, my honor won't let me tell you a thing," she said as she stood up and went to the mirror in his office. Then she began to run her hands through her hair and examine her face. "However, if you happened to be around while I was talking to myself, then that might work."

"Tap, tap, tap. I'm here tapping on my machine, working so hard."

Suahana laughed as she peered at him through the mirror.

"Really, I just want to freshen up before I see my friend. She so loves Vihaan that she was willing to leave him. Why, it was torture when I had to go to auntie and tell her Katherine had decided to leave so Vihaan wouldn't have to choose between her and the family. Such a loving and—"

Suhana didn't finish the sentence because she heard the running feet of Vihaan as he exited his office. She let out a sigh of relief and then turned around to look at the empty room. She'd done all she could do.

The knock on the door jarred Katherine out of her work. She had decided she would hide in her work until the pain went away. She wanted to leave the person at the door, but it might be a package from work, and she wouldn't let her personal issues get in the way of her work. The person knocked a little harder, and this time,

Katherine was going to give the postman a piece of her mind when she opened the door.

"Open, my queen, don't leave me on the steps to perish."

Katherine's hand was on the door as she let the warm tones wash over her. Vihaan? Of course it was Vihaan. The problem was, he shouldn't be outside her door. Was this the final nail in the coffin? She barely made it through the last time they spoke. She didn't know if she had it in her to make it through this time.

She opened up the door, and there he was. Any plan she had in her head to push him away fled from her mind. Her heart leaped with happiness on seeing him. She knew she was supposed to be scolding him and at the very least asking why was he here, but she couldn't. She just basked in his presence.

He still gave her tingles in her stomach. He was still the man that made her tuck her hair behind one ear, and her body always somehow shifted to its best viewpoint. Was she posing for him? She was in deep.

"Are we done hurting each other?" he asked as she stepped into the house.

"I don't know what you're talking about."

"We both let my aunt push us off our game. I was embarrassed and tried to ignore what had happened by making light of it. I thought you knew already how special you were. I was scared you'd hear her and rethink who we could be."

Katherine nibbled her lower lip. "Family is important to you."

He reached out and ran his hand along her ear until his hand had traced her jawline and tilted her chin up. "Real family yells loudly, but they do what is best for you.

I hope you know that our differences are what make us. I wasn't looking for me in a woman. I was looking for a woman who wanted me."

Katherine hiccuped. "I want to be with you, Vihaan. I mean, I'll still do the numbers, but for the rest, I'm open to negotiation."

"So to be clear, everything I said that day I meant. After I had said it, I thought 'she's going to ditch me.' I'm here now, and I'm asking if you will be with me."

Katherine looked into his brown eyes and nodded. She couldn't believe what was happening, much less how. When she thought there was no way, love made one.

She saw his head coming down, and she closed her eyes until she felt his lips touch hers. When his mouth brushed against hers, she welcomed him with open arms. His hands were on her shoulders, and she walked into his embrace. They stayed in each other's arms and just reveled in the feeling. Then he leaned back and looked her in the eye.

"Do you have the last roll of cloth?"

She said yes in a whisper. She asked him to wait, and then she brought out the cloth. It was an emerald green. He took the cloth and asked her to lift her arms, and he began to wrap it around her.

"I know this is done by women, and usually you have to be in your personals, but I thought this would be a great way to start our journey."

"Our journey?"

"Love is always a journey. It enriches the people in the relationship and feeds those around them. Green is the color of growth, vitality, and life." When he was done, he tucked the end under her arm, and she looked at him expectantly.

"Okay?"

"Green is the final color of offering. It means that I see you the way you are. I see you as the giver and creator of life. Would you dance with me?"

Katherine laughed nervously. "I'll fall."

Vihaan shook his head. "Don't fear. I have you."

She nodded shyly, and when she was about to comment on their lack of music, he began to hum. It was silly to dance to him humming. When she took the first two or three steps, it was stilted and clumsy, but she listened and rested her head on his chest. The swaying from right to left took over, and before she knew it, she was moving to a rhythm she knew. They were in perfect sync, and tears formed behind her eyelids.

She felt protected, cared for, and confident in herself to trust her feelings and to trust love.

Epilogue

Patrick Cunningham was desperate. That was the only thing that could make him come to a town called Sweet Blooms. He sat in a chair outside of what he hoped was the Mayor's office. The room was cool, and there wasn't anyone else in the room. He was still trying to understand the conversation he'd had with the secretary.

"I'm here to see the Mayor."

The secretary looked up at him and arched her brow.

"Do you have an appointment?"

Patrick wanted to look around the room and say there wasn't a need; no one wanted to see her but him. This was the price he was paying for falling into such dire straits. When he had gotten that tip on bitcoin, he went out and borrowed against his coop and put all of his meager savings in the tip and bought the bitcoin. It was a sure thing; the coin went up and down, they said. Well, his luck was in full swing because the week he invested, the stock market was strong, and bitcoin took a dive. Where once he was at a positive now, he was at a negative.

Bills were coming due, and he needed to recoup so

he could pull himself together. Just when he thought it was over, he went through his old mail and found a letter from a lawyer. It said his uncle owned land in a place called Sweet Bloom. It was about 6.5 acres. All Patrick could think of was that it would be enough to tide him over.

He maxed out what was left of his card and made it to Sweet Blooms.

"Excuse me, sir, do you have an appointment?"

Patrick bit his tongue and shook his head. "No."

"Well, then, take a seat, and I'll try to fit you in."

Patrick pasted a smile on his face and went back to his seat. *Fit me in? Fit me in between what?*

Just then, a woman walked into the room with a large watering can. The receptionist knew her.

"Daisy, I'm glad you came today. The plants are just awful without you. They miss you when you don't come."

The woman smiled and pushed back her blonde hair. Patrick didn't see her face when she walked in because the curtain of hair shielded her. She was in blue jeans that had seen some wear and tear and a large man's denim shirt with a white sleeveless tee shirt beneath. The t-shirt played peekaboo with the denim shirt. As she carried the large watering can, her denim shirt slipped off of her shoulder, showing tanned muscles that were used to being in the sun.

"Don't worry, I'll give the plants something extra," the woman said. Her voice was warm and soothing. He didn't know where she was from, but she had a slight lilt to her voice as if she wasn't from the small town of Sweet Blooms. Since he'd been here, he had heard twangs but no lilts.

Just when he thought he would think on his issues, she bent to put the can down, stood up, and tucked her hair behind her ears. Beautiful wasn't the word. With a natural tan, high cheekbones, and a mouth that formed a bow, she was forest nymph made real.

As if she felt his gaze, she turned to look at him. She looked at him from top to bottom and then turned away. He felt as if he had committed a faux pas but didn't know what it was. Then she grabbed her can and went into the office. It was a shame she had such a bad reaction to him. It didn't matter because he wasn't staying, but then something occurred to him, and he asked the receptionist, "If I'm waiting for the mayor, how come she can just go in?"

The receptionist looked at him, confused for a moment before she answered. "Daisy does the plants; of course she can go in the office. However, I wouldn't let anyone skip you. The mayor isn't in the office, so we are waiting."

I hope you enjoyed Katherine and Vihaan's story. Check out book Six in the Love Happens Series *Sweet Gamble* and read Patrick and Daisy's story.

Sign up to my newsletter to receive updates on new releases, sale promotions, and free books.

susanwarnerauthor.com

9 781948 377492